## THE PRICE OF SURVIVAL

Three men, all products of a star-spanning civilization, are irrevocably stranded on a primitive planet, a planet whose highest culture has not yet invented the wheel.

One goes mad.

One suicides.

Paul Marlowe survives—but the price is very high.

"[Edmund Cooper's] portrait of an alien culture and a man trying to deal with it is more than substantial . . ."

—*The Kirkus Service*

# A FAR SUNSET

by
**Edmund Cooper**

**ace books**

A Division of Charter Communications Inc.
A GROSSET & DUNLAP COMPANY
1120 Avenue of the Americas
New York, New York 10036

A FAR SUNSET

Copyright © 1967 by Edmund Cooper

An ACE book

First Ace printing: December 1977

*Cover art by David Bergen*

Printed in U.S.A.

# ONE

THE STAR SHIP blew itself to glory, as the three of them knew it would, on the thirty-fifth day of their imprisonment in the donjons of Baya Nor. If they had shared the same cell, they might have been able to help each other; but since the day of their capture they had been kept separate. Their only contacts had been the noia who lived with each of them and the guards who brought their food.

The explosion was like an earthquake. It shook the very foundations of Baya Nor. The god-king consulted his council, the council consulted the oracle; and the oracle consulted the sacred bones, shivered, went into a trance and emerged from it a considerable time later to announce that this was the signal of Oruri, that Oruri had marked Baya

Nor down for greatness, and that the coming of the strangers was a favourable omen.

The strangers themselves, however, knew nothing of these deliberations. They were incarcerated with their noias until they were rational enough—which meant until they had learned the language—to be admitted to the presence of the god-king.

Unfortunately the god-king, Enka Ne the 609th, was not destined to make the acquaintance of all of them; for the destruction of the star ship was a very traumatic experience. Each of the strangers wore an electronic watch, each of them had been able to keep a very accurate calendar. And each of them knew to the minute when the main computer would finally admit to itself that the crew had either abandoned the ship or were unable to return. At which point the main computer—for reasons obvious to the people who had built the vessel—was programmed to programme destruction. Which meant simply that the controls were lifted from the atomic generator. The rest would take care of itself.

Each of the strangers in his cell began a private countdown, at the same time hoping that one or more of the other nine members of the crew would return in time. None of them did. And so the star ship was transformed into a mushroom cloud, a circle of fire burnt itself out in the northern forests of Baya Nor, and a small glass-lined crater remained to commemorate the event.

In the donjons of Baya Nor, the second engineer went insane. He curled himself up into a tight foetal ball. But since he was not occupying a uterus, and since there was no umbilical cord to supply him with sustenance, and since the noia who was his only companion knew nothing at all about intravenous feeding, he eventually starved himself to death.

The chief navigator reacted with violence. He strangled his noia and then contrived to hang himself.

Oddly enough, the only member of the crew who managed to remain sane and survive was the star ship's psychiatrist. Being temperamentally inclined to pessimism, he had spent the last fifteen days of his captivity psychologically conditioning himself.

And so, when the donjons trembled, when his noia cowered under the bed and when in his mind's eye he saw the beautiful shape of the star ship convulsed instantly into a great ball of fire, he repeated to himself hypnotically: "My name is Poul Mer Lo. I am an alien. But this planet will be my home. This is where I must live and die. This is where I must now belong . . . My name is Poul Mer Lo. I am an alien. But this planet will be my home. This is where I must live and die. This is where I must now belong . . ."

Despite the tears that were running unnoticed down his cheeks, Poul Mer Lo felt extraordinarily calm. He looked at his noia, crouching under the bed. Though he did not yet perfectly understand the language, he realized that she was muttering incantations to ward off evil spirits.

Suddenly, he felt a strange and tremendous sense of pity.

"Mylai Tui," he said, addressing her formally.

"There is nothing to fear. What you have heard and felt is not the wrath of Oruri. It is something that I can understand, although I cannot explain it to you. It is something very sad, but without danger for you or your people."

Mylai Tui came out from under the bed. In thirty-five days and nights she had learned a great deal about Poul Mer Lo. She had given him her body, she had given him her thoughts, she had taught him the tongue of Baya Nor. She had laughed at his awkwardness and his stupidity. She had been surprised by his tenderness, and amazed by his friendship. Nobody—but nobody—ever acknowledged friendship for a simple noia.

Except the stranger, Poul Mer Lo.

"My lord weeps," she said uncertainly. "I take courage from the words of Poul Mer Lo. But his sadness is my sadness. Therefore I, too, must weep."

The psychiatrist looked at her, wondering how it would be possible to express himself in a language that did not appear to consist of more than a few hundred different words. He touched his face and was surprised to find tears.

"I weep," he said calmly, "because of the death of a great and beautiful bird. I weep because I am far from the land of my people, and I do not think that I shall ever return . . ." He hesitated. "But I rejoice, Mylai Tui, that I have known you. And I rejoice that I have discovered the people of Baya Nor."

The girl looked at him. "My lord has the gift of greatness," she said simply. "Surely the god-king will look on you and be wise."

4

# TWO

THAT EVENING, when at last he managed to get to sleep, Poul Mer Lo had nightmares. He dreamed that he was encased in a transparent tube. He dreamed that there was a heavy hoar frost all over his frozen body, covering even his eyes, choking his nostrils, sealing his stiff immovable lips. He dreamed also that he dreamed.

And in the dream within a dream there were rolling cornfields, rippling towards the horizon as far as the eye could see. There was a blue sky in which puffy white clouds drifted like fat good-natured animals browsing lazily on blue pastures.

There was a dwelling—a house with walls of whitened mud and crooked timbers and a roof of smoky yellow reeds. Suddenly he was inside the house. There was a table. His shoulder was just about as high as the table. He could see delicious mountains of food—all the things that he liked to eat best.

There were toys. One of them was a star ship on a launching pad. You set the ship on the launcher, cranked the little handle as far back as you could, then pressed the Go button. And off went the star ship like a silver bird.

The good giant, his father, said: "Happy birthday, my son."

The wicked witch, his mother, said: "Happy birthday, darling."

And suddenly he was back in the transparent tube, with the hoar frost sealing his lips so that he could neither laugh nor cry.

There was terror and coldness and loneliness.

The universe was nothing but a great ball of nothing, punctured by burning needle points, shot through with the all-embracing mirage of stillness and motion, of purpose and irrelevance.?

He had never known that silence could be so profound, that darkness could be so deep, that starlight could be so cold.

The universe dissolved.

There was a city, and in the city a restaurant, and in the restaurant a specimen of that vertical biped, the laughing mammal. She had hair the colour of the cornfields he remembered from childhood. She had eyes that were as blue as the skies of childhood. She had beautiful lips, and the sounds that came from them were like nothing at all in his childhood. Above all, she emanated warmth. She was the richness of high summer, the promise of a great sweet harvest.

She said: "So the world is not enough?" It was a question to which she already knew the answer.

He smiled. "You are enough, but the world is too small."

She toyed with her drink. "One last question, the classic question, and then we'll forget everything except this night . . . Why do you really have to go out to the stars?"

He was still smiling, but the smile was now mechanical. He didn't know. "There is the classic answer," he said evenly. "Because they are there."

"The moon is there. The planets are there. Isn't that enough?"

"People have been to the moon and the planets before me," he explained patiently. "That's why it's not enough."

"I think I could give you happiness," she whispered.

He took her hand. "I know you could."

"There could be children. Don't you want children?"

"I would like your children."

"Then have them. They're yours for the begetting."

"My love . . . Oh, my love . . . The trouble is I want something more."

She could not understand. She looked at him with bewilderment. "What is it? What is this thing that means more than love and happiness and children?"

He gazed at her, disconcerted. How to find the truth! How to find the words! And how to believe that the words could have anything at all to do with the truth.

"I want," he said with difficulty, and groping for the right images, "I want to be one of those who take the first steps. I want to leave a footprint on the farther shore." He laughed. "I even want to steal for myself a tiny fragment of history. Now tell me I'm paranoid. I'll believe you."

She stood up. "I've had my answer, and I'll tell you nothing," she said, "except that they're playing the Emperor Waltz . . . Do you want it?"

He wanted it.

They danced together in a lost bubble of time . . .

He wanted to cry. But how could you cry with frozen lips and frozen eyes and a frozen heart? How could you feel when you were locked in the bleak grip of eternity?

He woke up screaming.

The donjons of Baya Nor had not changed. The black-haired, wide-eyed noia by his side had not changed. Only he had changed because the conditioning—thank God—had failed. Because men were men and not machines. Because the grief inside him was so deep and so desolate that he, who had always considered himself to be nothing more than a blue-eyed computer, at last knew what it was to be a terrified animal.

He sat up in bed, eyes staring, the hairs at the nape of his neck twitching and stiffening.

"My name is Paul Marlowe," he babbled in words that his noia could not understand. "I am a native of Earth and I have aged four years in the last twenty years. I have sinned against the laws of life." He held his head in his hands, rocking to and fro. "Oh God! Punish me with pain that I can bear. Chastize me! Strip the flesh from my back. Only give me back the world I threw away!"

Then he collapsed, sobbing.

The noia cradled his head upon her breast.

"My lord has many visions," she murmured. "Visions are hard to bear, but they are the gift of Oruri and so must be borne. Know then, Poul Mer Lo, my lord, that your servant would ease the burden if Oruri so decrees."

Poul Mer Lo raised his head and looked at her. He pulled himself together. "Do not sorrow," he said in passable Bayani. "I have been troubled by dreams. I grieve only for the death of a child long ago."

Mylai Tui was puzzled. "My lord, first there was the death of a great bird, and now there is the death of a child. Surely there is too much of dying in your heart?"

Poul Mer Lo smiled. "You are right. There is too much dying. It seems that I must learn to live again."

# THREE

IN THE YEAR 2012 A.D. (local time) three star ships left Sol Three, known more familiarly to its inhabitants as Earth. The first star ship to venture out into the deep black yonder was—inevitably—the American vessel *Mayflower*. It was (and in this even the Russian and European inspection engineers agreed) the most ambitious, the largest and possibly the most beautiful machine ever devised by man. It had taken ten years, thirty billion new dollars and nine hundred and fourteen lives to assemble in the two-hour orbit. It was built to contain forty-five pairs of human beings and its destination was the Sirius system.

The second star ship to leave Sol Three was the Russian vessel *Red October*. Though not as large as the American ship it was (so the American and European inspection engineers concluded) somewhat faster. It, too, was expensive and beautiful. It, too, had cost many lives. The Russians, despite everyone's scepticism, had managed to assemble it in the three hour orbit in a mere six years. It was built to contain twenty-seven men and twenty-seven women (unpaired), and its destination was Procyon.

The third ship to leave was the *Gloria Mundi*. It had been built on a relative shoe-string in the ninety-minute orbit by the new United States of Europe. It was called the *Gloria Mundi* because the Germans would not agree to an English name, the French would not agree to a German name, the English would not agree to a French name and the Italians could not even agree among themselves on a name. So a name drawn from the words of a dead language was the obvious answer. And because the ship was the smallest of the vessels, its chief architect—an Englishman with a very English sense of humour—had suggested calling it The Glory of the World. It was designed to carry six pairs of human beings: one German pair, one French pair, one British pair, one Italian pair, one Swedish pair and one Dutch pair. It was smaller than the Russian ship and slower than the American ship. Inevitably its target star was farther away than either the American or the Russian target stars. It was bound for Altair—a matter of sixteen light-years or nearly twenty-one years, ship's time.

In the twenty-first century the British sense of propriety was still a force to be reckoned with.

That is why, on the morning of April 3rd 2012 A.D. Paul Marlowe, wearing a red rose in the button hole of his morning coat, appeared punctually at Caxton Hall registry office at 10.30 a.m. At 10.35 a.m. Ann Victoria Watkins appeared. By 10.50 a.m. the couple had been pronounced man and wife. It was estimated that three hundred million people witnessed the ceremony over Eurovision.

Paul and Ann did not like each other particularly: nor did they dislike each other. But as the British contribution to the crew of the *Gloria Mundi* they accepted their pairing with good grace. Paul, a trained space-hand, possessed the skills of psychiatry and teaching and was also fluent in French and German. Ann's dowry was medicine and surgery, a working knowledge of Swedish and Italian and enough Dutch to make conversation under pressure.

After the ceremony they took a taxi to Victoria, a hover train to Gatwick, a strato-rocket to Woomera and then a ferry capsule to the ninety-minute orbit. They spent their honeymoon working through the pre-jump routines aboard the *Gloria Mundi*.

Despite many differences in size, design and accommodation, the American, Russian and European space ships all had one thing in common. They all contained sleeper units for the crews. None of the ships could travel faster than light— though the Russians claimed that given theoretically ideal conditions *Red October* could just pass the barrier—so their occupants were doomed to many years of star travel; during which it was a statistical certainty that some would die, go mad,

12

mutiny or find even more ingenious ways of becoming useless. Unless they had sleeper units.

Suspended animation had been developed years before in the closing decades of the twentieth century. At first it had been used in a very limited way for heart transplants. Then someone had discovered that the simple process of freezing a neurotic for a period of days or weeks, depending on the degree of neurosis, could produce an almost complete cure. Then someone else hit upon the idea of using suspended animation for the insane, the incurable or the dying. Such people, it was argued, could be frozen for decades if necessary until an answer was found for their particular malady.

By the beginning of the twenty-first century, suspended animation had become an integral part of the way of life of every civilized community. Not only the seriously ill and the seriously mad were frozen. Criminals were frozen, suspended animation sentences ranging from one to fifty years, depending on the seriousness of the crime. And rich citizens, who had lived most of their lives and exhausted all the conventional rejuvenation techniques would go voluntarily into indefinite suspended animation in the sublime hope that one day somebody would discover the secret of immortality. Even the dead, if they were important enough and if they could be obtained soon after the point of clinical death, were frozen—on the theory that a few more decades would bring great advances in resurrection techniques.

But whatever the value of suspended animation was for those who hoped to cheat death, the asylum, the executioner or the normal laws of existence, it was certainly the ideal form of travelling for those who were destined to venture into deep space.

It was estimated that the *Gloria Mundi* could not possibly reach Altair in less than twenty years of subjective time. Therefore a programme of rotational suspended animation had been worked out for the crew. For the first three months of the voyage all crew members would be live and operational. For the rest of the voyage, with the exception of the last three months, each pair would, in turn, remain live for one month (terrestrial time) and then be suspended for five. In case of an emergency all five frozen pairs (or any individual whose special skill was required) could be defrozen in ten hours.

During the course of the long and uneventful voyage to Altair, Paul Marlowe spent a total of nearly four working years in the company of his "wife". He never got to know her. As a psychiatrist, he would have thought that the absolute isolation of a long space voyage would have been bound to bring two people intimately together. But he never got to know her.

She had dark hair, an attractive face and a pleasant enough body. They made love quite a lot of times during their waking months. They shared jokes, they discussed books, they watched old films together. But somehow she was too dedicated, too remote. And he never really got to know her.

That, perhaps, was why he could summon no tears, could feel no personal sense of loss when she finally disappeared on Altair Five.

# FOUR

MORNING SUNLIGHT poured through four of the
sixteen small glassless windows of the donjon.
Poul Mer Lo was sleeping. The noia did not waken
him. Clearly he had been touched by Oruri. He
needed to sleep.

As always she marvelled at the stature and ap-
pearance of the outlander. He was half as high
again as Mylai Tui, who was reckoned exceedingly
tall—and therefore ugly—by her own people. His
skin was interestingly pale, whereas hers was
brown and almost, indeed, the prized black of the
Bayani of ancient lineage. His eyes, when they
were open, were light blue—a wondrous colour,
since all Bayani eyes were either brown or ochre.
The muscles in his arms and legs were like the
muscles of a powerful animal. Which was strange

since, though he was clearly a barbarian, he was a man of some sensibility. He was also very much a man; for she, who had experienced many vigorous Bayani as a priestess in the Temple of Gaiety, had found to her surprise that she could only accommodate his thanu with difficulty. The effort was at times painful: but also, at times, it produced joy greater even than the condescension of Oruri.

She shrank back from the mental blasphemy, shutting it out. Nevertheless she took joy in the remembered frenzies of Poul Mer Lo. Apart from the facts that his nose was rather sharp and his ears seemed to be imperfectly joined to his head his only serious malformation was that he had too many fingers.

Poul Mer Lo stirred and yawned. Then he opened his eyes.

"Greetings, my lord," said Mylai Tui formally. "Oruri has bestowed upon us the blessing of another day."

"Greetings, Mylai Tui." He was getting familiar with the customs as well as with the language. "The blessing is ill deserved." But the words were mechanical and the look in his eyes was blank. Or far away. Far, far away . . .

"Soon we shall eat and drink," she went on, hoping to bring him back to reality. "Soon we shall walk in the garden."

"Yes." Poul Mer Lo did not move. He lay on his back despondently, staring at the ceiling.

"My lord," said Mylai Tui desperately, "tell me again the story of the silver bird. It is one that is most beautiful to hear."

"You already know the story of the silver bird."

16

He did not look at her, but laughed bitterly. "You probably know it better than I do."

"Nevertheless, I would hear it once more . . . If my ears are still worthy."

Poul Mer Lo sighed and raised himself on one arm, but still he did not look at her.

"There is a land beyond the sky," he began. "It is a land filled with many people who are skilled in the working of metal. It is a land where men do not know the laws of Oruri. It is a land where people may talk to each other and see each other at a great distance. It is truly a land of miracles. Among the people of this land there are some who are very wise and also very skilled and very ambitious. They have looked at the night sky and said to themselves: 'Truly the stars are far from us, yet they tempt us. Shall we not seek ways of reaching them so that we may know what they are like?' "

Mylai Tui shivered and, as always at this point, interrupted. "Such men," she pronounced, "must not only be brave and mad. They must also be most eager to accept the embrace of Oruri."

"They do not know the laws of Oruri," pointed out Poul Mer Lo patiently. "They hunger only for knowledge and power . . . So it was that they dreamed of building a flock of silver birds whereon their young men and women might ride out to the stars."

"It was the old ones who should have made the journey, for their time was near."

"Nevertheless, it was the young ones who were chosen. For it was known that the stars were far away and that the flight of the silver birds would last many seasons."

"Then the young ones would grow old on the journey."

"No. The young ones did not grow old. For the wise men had found ways of making them sleep for the greater part of the journey."

"My lord," said Mylai Tui, "those who sleep too much also starve."

"These did not starve," retorted Poul Mer Lo, "for their sleep was deeper than any living sleep that is known in Baya Nor . . . You have asked for the story, noia, so let me tell it; otherwise neither of us will be content."

Mylai Tui was saddened. He only addressed her as noia—knowing that it was incorrect—when he was angry.

"I am reproved by Poul Mer Lo," she said gravely. "It is just."

"Well, then. Three silver birds left the land beyond the sky, each of them bound upon a different journey. I and eleven companions were chosen to ride the last and smallest of the birds. We were bound for the star that you know as the sun of Baya Nor. The wise men told us that the flight would take twenty or more cool seasons . . . We journeyed, most of us sleeping, but some always watching. As we came near to this star we saw that it shone brightly on a fair world, the world of Baya Nor. To us who had ridden upon the silver bird through a great darkness for so many seasons, the land of Baya Nor seemed very beautiful. We directed the bird to set us down so that we might see what manner of people lived here. Nine of our party set out to wander through your forests and did not return. After many days, we who were left decided to look for them. We did not find them. We found only the darts of your hunters and the donjons of Baya Nor . . . Because no one returned to set the bird upon its homeward journey, it destroyed itself by fire." Poul Mer Lo suddenly looked at her and smiled. "And so, Mylai Tui, I am here and you are here; and together we must make the best of it."

The noia let out a deep breath. "It is a sweet and sad story," she said simply. "And I am glad, my lord, that you came. I am glad that I have known you."

Outside there were sounds of marching feet. Presently the bars were taken from the door. Two slaves, watched by two guards, entered the donjon with platters of food and pitchers of water.

But Poul Mer Lo was not hungry.

# FIVE

THE *GLORIA MUNDI* had gone into the thousand
kilometre orbit round Altair Five. Further out in
solar space other satellites were detected; but they
had been rotating around the planet somewhat
longer than the terrestrial vessel and they were
untenanted. They were nothing more than great
dead lumps of rock—the nine moons of Altair Five
that had once, perhaps, been a single moon. To the
naked eye they were large enough to reveal themselves as a flock of large and apparently mobile
stars.

The planet itself was a miracle. Statistically it
was the jackpot, for the occupants of the *Gloria
Mundi* could not bring themselves to believe
that—in a cosmos so empty, yet whose material

content was so diverse—either of the other terrestrial vessels could have encountered an earthtype planet. The odds were greater, as the Swedish physicist succinctly put it, than the chance of dealing four consecutive suits from a shuffled pack of playing cards.

Altair Five was not only earth-type; it was oddly symmetrical and—to people who had conditioned themselves to expect nothing but barren worlds or, at best, planets inhabited by life forms that were low in the biological series—quite beautiful. It was slightly smaller than Mars and nine tenths of it was ocean, spotted here and there by a few small colonies of islands. But there was quite a large north polar continent and an almost identical south polar continent. But, most interesting of all, there was a broad horseshoe of a continent stretching round the equatorial region, one end of it separated from the other by a few hundred kilometres of water.

The polar continents were covered for the most part by eternal snows and ice; but the great mass of equatorial land displayed nearly all the features that might be observed on the terrestrial continent of Africa from a similar altitude.

There were mountains and deserts, great lakes, bush and tropical rain forests. Under the heat of the sun, the deserts burned with fiery, iridescent hues of yellow and orange and red; the mountains were brown, freckled with blue and white; the bush was a scorched amber; and the rain forests seemed to glow with a subtle pot-pourri of greens and turquoises.

The planet rotated on its own axis once every

twenty-eight hours and seventeen minutes terrestrial time. Calculations showed that it would complete one orbit round Altair, its sun, in four hundred and two local days.

The life of the planet was clearly based upon the carbon cycle; and an analysis of its atmosphere showed only that there was a slightly higher proportion of nitrogen than in that of Sol Three.

The *Gloria Mundi* stayed in the thousand kilometre orbit for four hundred and ten revolutions or approximately twenty terrestrial days. During that time every aspect of the planet was photographed and telephotographed. In one section of the equatorial continent, the photographs revealed the classic sign of occupation by intelligent beings—irrigation or, just possibly, transport canals.

The occupants of the *Gloria Mundi* experienced sensations akin to ecstasy. They had endured confinement, synthetic hibernation and the black star-pricked monotony of a deep space voyage; they had crossed sixteen light-years in sixteen years of suspended animation and over four years of waking and ageing. And at the end of it their privation and endurance had been rewarded by the best of all possible finds—a world in which people lived. Whether they were people with four eyes and six legs did not matter. What mattered was that they were intelligent and creative. With beings of such calibre it would surely be possible to establish fruitful communication.

The *Gloria Mundi* touched down within twenty kilometres of the nearest canals. With such a large ship—and bearing in mind that the German pilot had only experienced planetary manoeuvers of the vessel in simulation—it was a feat of considerable skill. The vessel burned a ten-kilometre swathe through the luxuriant forest then sat neatly on its tail while the four stability shoes groped gently through the smouldering earth for bedrock. They found it less than five metres down.

For the first three planetary days, nobody went outside the vessel. Vicinity tests were conducted. At the end of three days the airlock was opened and two armoured volunteers descended by nylon ladder into a forest that was already beginning to cover the scars of its great burning. The volunteers stayed outside for three hours, collecting samples but never straying more than a few metres from the base of the ship. One of them shot and killed a large snake that seemed to exhibit the characteristics of a terrestrial boa.

On the ninth day of planetfall an exploration team consisting of the Swedish pair, the French pair and the Dutch pair set out. Each of the members of the team wore thigh length boots, plastic body armour and a light plastic visor. The temperature was far too high for them to wear more—other than fully armoured and insulated and altogether restricting space suits.

The women carried automatic sweeper rifles: the men carried nitro-pistols and atomic grenade throwers. All of them carried transceivers. Between them they had enough fire-power to dispose of a twentieth-century armoured corps.

Their instructions were to complete a semi-circular traverse in the planetary east at a radius of five kilometres, to maintain radio contact every fifteen terrestrial minutes and to return within three planetary days.

All went well for the first planetary day and night. They encountered and reported many interesting animals and birds, but no sign of intelligent beings. In the middle of the second planetary day, radio communication ceased. At the end of the third day, the team did not return.

Six people, tormented by anxiety, were left aboard the *Gloria Mundi*. At the end of the fifteenth day of planetfall, a rescue team consisting of the three remaining women set out. They, too, carried nitro-pistols and grenade throwers.

The fact that it was the women who went and not the men was not fortuitous. Of the men who remained, two were vital to the running of the ship (assuming no success in rescue) if it was ever to return to Earth; and the third, Paul Marlowe, was suffering from a form of acute dysentery.

He said goodbye Dr. Ann Victoria Marlowe, née Watkins, without emotion. He was too ill to care: she was too clinical to be involved. After she had gone, he lay back on his bed, tried to forget his own exhausting symptoms and the world of Altair Five and to lose himself in a micro-film of one of the novels of Charles Dickens.

The rescue team maintained radio contact for no more than seven hours. Then it, too, became silent.

After four days, Paul Marlowe was over the worst of his dysentery; and he and his two companions were in a state of extreme depression.

They considered waiting in the citadel of the *Gloria Mundi* indefinitely; they considered pulling

back into orbit; they even considered heading out
of the system and back to Sol Three. For clearly
there was something badly wrong on Altair Five.

In the end they did none of those things. In the
end they decided to become a death-or-glory
squad.

It was Paul Marlowe, the psychiatrist, who
worked the problem out logically. Three people
were necessary to manage the ship. Therefore
there was no point in sending one or two men out if
he or they failed to return. For the vessel would
still be grounded. So they must either all go or all
stay. If they stayed in the *Gloria Mundi* and eventually returned to Sol Three, they would lose their
self-respect—in much the same manner as moun-
taineers who have been forced to cut the rope. If,
on the other hand, they formed themselves into a
second search party and failed, they would have
betrayed the trust vested in them by all the people
of the United States of Europe.

But the United States of Europe was sixteen
light-years away and under the present circumstances, their duty to such a remote concept was
itself a remote abstraction. What mattered more
were the people with whom they had shared
danger and monotony and triumph—and now disaster.

So, really, there was no choice. They had to go.

By this time the ship's armoury was sadly de-
pleted; but there were still enough weapons left for
the three men to give a respectable account of
themselves if they were challenged by a visible
enemy. On the twentieth day of planetfall they
emerged from the womb-like security of the *Gloria*

*Mundi* to be born again—as Paul Marlowe saw it imaginatively—into an unknown but thoroughly hostile environment.

The designers of the *Gloria Mundi* had tried to foresee every possible emergency that could occur—including the death, disappearance, defection or defeat of the entire crew. If by any remote possibility, it was argued, such types of catastrophe occurred on a planet with sophisticated inhabitants, it would theoretically be possible for the said inhabitants to take over the ship, check the star maps, track back on the log and the computer programmes and—defying all laws of probability, but subscribing to the more obtuse laws of absurdity—return the *Gloria Mundi* to Earth.

That, in itself, might be a good and charitable act. Or, depending on the nature, the potential and the intentions of the aliens who accomplished it, it might by some remote chance be the worst thing that could possibly happen to the human race. Whatever the result of such highly theoretical speculations could turn out to be, the designers were of the opinion—wholeheartedly endorsed by their respective governments—that they could not afford to take chances.

Consequently the *Gloria Mundi* had been programmed to destroy herself on the thirty-fifth day of her abandonment—if that disastrous event ever took place. Thirty-five days, it was argued, ought to be long enough to resolve whatever crisis confronted the crew. If it wasn't, then the *Gloria Mundi* and all who travelled in her would have to be a write-off.

The designers were very logical people. Some had argued for a twenty-day limit and some had argued for a ninety-day limit. Absorbed as they were in abstractions, few of them had paid much attention to the human element, and none of them could have foreseen the situation on Altair Five.

By the evening of the twentieth day of planetfall, the three remaining crew members had covered about seven kilometres of their search through the barely penetrable forests and had found not the slighest trace of their companions. They had just set up a circle of small but powerful electric lamps and an inner perimeter of electrified alarm wire behind which they proposed to bivouac for the night when Paul Marlowe felt a stinging sensation in his knee.

He turned to speak to his two companions, but before he could do so he fell unconscious to the ground.

Later he woke up in what was, though he did not then know it, one of the donjons of Baya Nor.

Much later, in fact thirty-three days later, the *Gloria Mundi* turned into a high and briefly terrible mushroom of flame and radiant energy.

# SIX

It WAS mid-morning; and Poul Mer Lo, surrounded by small dancing rainbows, drenched by a
fine water mist, was kneeling with his arms tied
behind his back. Behind him stood two Bayani
warriors, each armed with a short trident, each
trident poised above his neck for a finishing stroke.
Before him lay the sad heap of his personal possessions: one electronic wristwatch, one miniature
transceiver, one vest, one shirt, one pair of shorts,
one plastic visor, a set of body armour, a pair of
boots and an automatic sweeper rifle.

Poul Mer Lo was naked. The mist formed into
refreshing droplets on his body, the droplets ran
down his face and chest and back. The Bayani
warriors stood motionless. There was nothing to

be heard but the hypnotic sound of the fountains. There was nothing to do but wait patiently for his audience with the god-king.

He looked at the sweeper rifle and smiled. It was a formidable weapon. With it—and providing he could choose his ground—he could annihilate a thousand Bayani armed with tridents. But he had not been able to choose his ground. And here he was—at the mercy of two small brown men, awaiting the pleasure of the god-king of Baya Nor.

He wanted to laugh. He badly wanted to laugh. But he repressed the laughter because his motivation might have been misunderstood. The two sombre guards could hardly be expected to appreciate the irony of the situation. To them he was simply a stranger, a captive. That he could be an emissary from a technological civilization on another world would be utterly beyond their comprehension.

In the country of the blind, thought Poul Mer Lo, recalling a legend that belonged to another time and space, the one-eyed man is king.

Again he wanted to laugh. For, as in the legend, the blind men—with all their obvious limitations—had turned out to be more formidable than the man with one eye.

"You are smiling," said an oddly immature voice. "There are not many who dare to smile in the presence. Nor are there many who do not even notice the presence."

Poul Mer Lo blinked the droplets from his eyes and looked up. At first he thought he saw a great bird, covered in brilliant plumage, with iridescent feathers of blue and red and green and gold; and with brilliant yellow eyes and a hooked black beak. But the feathers clothed a man, and the great bird's head was set like a helmet above a recognisable face. The face of Enka Ne, god-king of Baya Nor.

It was also the face of a boy—or of a very young man.

"Lord," said Poul Mer Lo, struggling now with the language that had seemed so easy when he practised it with the noia, "I ask pardon. My thoughts were far away."

"Riding, perhaps, on the wings of a silver bird," suggested Enka Ne, "to a land beyond the sky . . . Yes, I have spoken with the noia. You have told her a strange story . . . It is the truth?"

"Yes, Lord, it is the truth."

Enka Ne smiled. "Here we have a story about a beast called a tlamyn. It is supposed to be a beast of the night, living in caves and dark places, never showing itself by day. It is said that once long ago six of our wise men ventured into the lair of a tlamyn—not, indeed, knowing of the presence or even the existence of such a creature. One of the wise men chanced upon the tlamyn's face. It was tusked and hard and hairy like the dongoir that we hunt for sport. Therefore, feeling it in the darkness, he concluded that he had encountered a dongoir. Another touched the soft underbelly. It had two enormous breasts. Therefore, he concluded that he had come upon a great sleeping woman. A third touched the beast's legs. They had scales and claws. Naturally, he thought he had found a nesting bird. A fourth touched the tlamyn's tail. It was long and muscular and cold. So he decided that he had stumbled across a great serpent. A fifth found a pair of soft ears and deduced that he was lucky enough to discover one of the domasi whose meat we prize. And the sixth, sniffing the scent of the tlamyn, thought that he must be in the Temple of Gaiety. Each of the wise men made his discovery known to his comrades. Each insisted that his interpretation was the truth. The noise of their disputation, which was prolonged and energetic, eventually woke the sleeping tlamyn. And it, being very hungry, promptly ate them all . . . I should add that none of my people have ever seen a tlamyn and lived.''

Poul Mer Lo looked at the god-king, surprised by his intelligence. ''Lord, that was a good story. There is one like it, concerning a creature called an elephant, that is told in my own country.''

''In the land beyond the sky?''

''In the land beyond the sky.''

Enka Ne laughed. ''What is truth?'' he demanded. ''Beyond the world in which we live there is nothing but Oruri. And even I am but a passing shadow in his endless dreams.''

Pour Mer Lo decided to take a gamble. ''Yet who can say what and what does not belong to the dreams of Oruri. Might not Oruri dream of a strange country wherein there are such things as silver birds?''

Enka Ne was silent. He folded his arms, and gazed thoughtfully down at his prisoner. The feathers rustled. Water ran from them and made little pools on the stone floor.

At last the god-king spoke. "The oracle has said that you are a teacher—a great teacher. Is that so?"

"Lord, I have skills that were prized among my own people. I have a little of the knowledge of my people. I do not know if I am a great teacher. I do not yet know what I can teach."

The answer seemed to please Enka Ne. "Perhaps you speak honestly . . . Why did your comrades die?"

Until then, Poul Mer Lo had not known that he was the last survivor. He felt an intense desolation. He felt a sense of loneliness that made him cry out, as in pain.

"You suffer?" enquired the god-king. He looked puzzled.

Poul Mer Lo spoke with difficulty. "I did not know that my comrades were dead."

Again there was a silence. Enka Ne gazed disconcertingly at the pale giant kneeling before him. He moved from side to side as if inspecting the phenomenon from all possible angles. The feathers rustled. The noise of the fountains became loud, like thunder.

Eventually, the god-king seemed to have made up his mind.

"What would you do," asked Enka Ne, "if I were to grant you freedom?"

"I should have to find somewhere to stay."

"What would you do, then, if you found somewhere to stay?"

"I should have to find someone to cook for me. I do not even know what is good and what is not good to eat."

"And having found a home and a woman, what then?"

"Then, Lord, I should have to decide how I could repay the people of Baya Nor who have given me these things."

Enka Ne stretched out a hand. "Live," he said simply.

Poul Mer Lo felt a sharp jerk. Then his arms were free. The two silent Bayani warriors lifted him to his feet. He fell down because, having kneeled so long, the blood was not flowing in his legs.

Again they lifted him and supported him.

Enka Ne gazed at him without expression. Then he turned and walked away. After three or four paces he stopped and turned again.

He glanced at Poul Mer Lo and spoke to the guards. "This man has too many fingers," he said. "It is offensive to Oruri. Strike one from each hand."

# SEVEN

POUL MER LO was given a small thatched house that stood on short stilts just outside the sacred city, the noia with whom he had spent his imprisonment, and sixty-four copper rings. He did not know the value of the ring money; but Mylai Tui calculated that if he did not receive any further benefits from the god-king he could still live for nearly three hundred days without having to hunt or work for himself.

Poul Mer Lo thought the god-king had been more than generous, for he had provided the stranger with enough money to last his own lifetime. Wisely, perhaps, Enka Ne had not shown too much favour. He had made sure that Enka Ne the 610th would not be embarrassed by the munificence of his predecessor.

The little finger on each hand had been struck off expertly, the scars had healed and the only pain that remained was from tiny fragments of bone working their way slowly to the surface. Sometimes, when the weather was heavy, Poul Mer Lo was conscious of a throbbing. But, for the most part he had adjusted to the loss very well. It was quite remarkable how easily one could perform with only four fingers the tasks that had formerly required five.

For many days after he had received what amounted to the royal pardon, Poul Mer Lo spent his time doing nothing but learning. He walked abroad in the streets of Baya Nor and was surprised to find that he was, for the most part, ignored by the ordinary citizens. When he engaged them in conversation, his questions were answered politely; but none asked questions in return. The fate of a pygmy in the streets of London, he reflected, would very likely have been somewhat different. The fate of an extra-terrestrial in the streets of any terrestrial city would have been markedly different. Police would have been required to control the crowds—and, perhaps, disperse the lynch mobs. The more he learned, the more, he realized, he had to learn.

The population of Baya Nor, a city set in the midst of the forest, consisted of less than twenty thousand people. Of these nearly a third were farmers and craftsmen and rather more than a third were hunters and soldiers. Of the remainder, above five thousand priests maintained the temples and the waterways and about one thousand priest/lawyer/civil servants ran the city's administration. The god-king, Enka Ne, supported by a city council and an hereditary female oracle, reigned with all the powers of a despot for one year of four hundred days—at the end of which time he was sacrificed in the Temple of the Weeping Sun while the new god-king was simultaneously ordained.

Baya Nor itself was a city of water and stone— like a great Gothic lido, thought Poul Mer Lo, dropped crazily in the middle of the wilderness. The Bayani worshipped water, perhaps because water was the very fluid of life. There were reservoirs, pools and fountains everywhere. The main thoroughfares were broad waterways, so broad that they must have taken generations to construct. In each of the four main reservoirs, temples shaped curiously like pyramids rose hazily behind a wall of fountains to the blue sky. The temples too, were not such as could have been raised by a population of twenty thousand in less than a century. They looked very old, and they looked also as if they would endure longer than the race that built them.

In a literal and a symbolic sense Baya Nor was two cities—one within the other. The sacred city occupied a large island in the lake that was called the Mirror of Oruri. It was connected to the outer city by four narrow causeways, on each side of which were identical carvings representing all the god-kings since time immemorial.

If Baya Nor was not strong in science, it was certainly strong in art; for the generation of sculptors and masons who had carved the city out

of dark warm sandstone had left behind them
monuments of grandeur and classic line. Disdain-
ing a written language, they had composed their
common testament eloquently in a language of
form and composition. They had married water to
stone and had produced a living mobile poetry of
fountains and sunlight and shadow and sandstone
that was a song of joy to the greater glory of Oruri.

Poul Mer Lo knew little of the religion of the
Bayani. But as he surveyed its outward forms, he
could feel himself coming under its spell, could
sense the mystery that bound a people together in
the undoubted knowledge that their ideas, their
philosophy and their way of life were the most
perfect expression of the mystery of existence.

At times, Poul Mer Lo was frightened; knowing
that if he were to live and remain sane he would
have to assume to some extent the role of serpent
in this sophisticated yet oddly static Eden. He
would have to be himself—no longer an Earth
man, and not a man of Baya Nor. But a man poised
dreadfully between two worlds. A man chastened
by light-years, whipped by memories, haunted by
knowledge. A man pinned by circumstances to a
speck of cosmic dust far from that other speck he
had once called home. A man who, above all,
needed to talk, to make confession. A man with a
dual purpose—to create and to destroy.

At times he revelled in his purpose. At times he
was ashamed. At times, also, he remembered
someone who had once been called Paul Marlowe.
He remembered the prejudices and convictions
and compulsions that this strange person had

held. He remembered his arrogance and his certainty—his burning ambition to journey out to the stars.

Paul Marlowe had fulfilled that ambition, but in fulfilling it he had died. Alas for Paul Marlowe, who had never realized that it was possible to pay a greater price for private luxuries than either death or pain.

Paul Marlowe, native of Earth, had accomplished more than Eric the Red, Marco Polo, Columbus or even Darwin. But it was Poul Mer Lo, grace and favour subject of Enka Ne, who paid the price for his achievement.

And the price was absolute loneliness.

# EIGHT

THE HALF-STARVED youth, clad in a threadbare samu, who climbed up the steps as Poul Mer Lo watched from his verandah, seemed vaguely familiar. But though there were not many beggars in Baya Nor, their faces all looked the same—like those of the proverbial Chinamen to people on the other side of a world on the other side of the sky.

"Oruri greets you," said the youth, neglecting to hold out his begging bowl.

"The greeting is a blessing," retorted Poul Mer Lo automatically. After two fifty-day Bayani months, he found ritual conversation quite easy. According to form, the youth should now tell of the nobility of his grandfather, the virility of his father, the selfless devotion of his mother and the disaster that Oruri had inflicted upon them all to bring joy through penitence.

But the boy did not launch into the expected formula. He said: "Blessed also are they who have known many wonders. I may speak with you?"

Suddenly, Poul Mer Lo, who had been sitting cross-legged with Mylai Tui, enjoying the light evening breeze, recognized the voice. He sprang to his feet.

"Lord, I did not—"

"*Do not recognize me!*" The words shot out imperiously. Then the boy relaxed, and carried on almost apologetically: "I am Shah Shan, of late a waterman. I may speak with you?"

"Yes, Shah Shan, you may speak with me. I am Poul Mer Lo, a stranger now and always."

The boy smiled and held out his begging bowl. "Oruri has seen fit to grace me with a slight hunger. Perhaps he foresaw our meeting."

Silently, Mylai Tui rose to her feet, took the bowl and disappeared into the house. Poul Mer Lo watched her curiously. She had seemed almost not to see Shah Shan at all.

"Poul Mer Lo is gracious," said the boy. "It is permitted to sit?"

"It is permitted to sit," returned Poul Mer Lo gravely.

The two of them sat cross-legged on the veran- dah, and there was silence. Presently Mylai Tui returned with the bowl. It contained a small quan- tity of kappa, the cereal that was the staple diet of the poor and that the prosperous only ate with meat and vegetables.

Shah Shan took the kappa and ate it greedily

with his fingers. When he had finished, he belched politely.

"I have a friend," he said, "whose head has been troubled with dreams and strange thoughts. I think that you may help him."

"I am sorry for your friend. I do not know that I can help him, but if he comes to me, I will try."

"The kappa is still green," said Shah Shan.

Poul Mer Lo was familiar enough with idiomatic Bayani to understand that the time was not ripe.

"My friend is of some importance," went on the boy. "He has much to occupy him. Nevertheless, he is troubled . . . See, I will show you something that he has shown me."

Shah Shan rose to his feet, went down the verandah steps and found a small stick. He proceeded to draw in the dust.

Poul Mer Lo watched him, astounded.

Shah Shan had drawn the outline of the *Gloria Mundi*.

"My friend calls this a silver bird," he explained. "But it does not look like a bird. Can you explain this?"

"It is truly a silver bird. It is a—a—" Poul Mer Lo floundered. There was no Bayani word for machine, or none that he knew. "It was fashioned by men in metal," he said at last, "as a sculptor fashions in stone. It brought me to your world."

"There is another thing," continued Shah Shan. "My friend has seen the silver bird passing swiftly round a great ball. The ball was very strange. It was not a ball of yarn such as the children play with. It was a ball of water. And there was some land on which forests grew. And in the forests there were waterways. Also there was a city with many temples and four great reservoirs . . . My friend was disturbed."

Poul Mer Lo was even more amazed. "Your friend need not be disturbed," he said at length. "He saw truly what has happened. The great ball is your world. The reservoirs are those of Baya Nor . . . Your friend has had a very wonderful dream."

Shah Shan shook his head. "My friend has a sickness. The world is flat—flat as the face of water when there is no wind. It is known that if a man journeys far—if he is mad enough to journey far—from Baya Nor, he will fall off the edge of the world. Perhaps if he is worthy, he will fall on to the bosom of Oruri. Otherwise there can be no end to his falling."

Poul Mer Lo was silent for a moment or two. Then he said hesitantly: "Shah Shan, I too have a friend who seems wise though he is still very young. He told me a story about six men who found a sleeping tlamyn. Each of the men thought the tlamyn was something else. Eventually, they argued so much that it woke up and ate them."

"I have heard the story," said Shah Shan gravely. "It is amusing."

"The tlamyn is truth. It is not given to men to understand truth completely. However wise they are, they are only permitted to see a little of the truth. But may not some see more than others?"

Shah Shan's forehead wrinkled. "It is possible," he said presently, "that a stranger to this land may see a different countenance of the truth

. . . A stranger who has journeyed far and therefore witnessed many happenings.''

Poul Mer Lo was encouraged. ''You speak wisely. Listen, then, to the strange thoughts of a stranger. Time is divided into day and night, is it not? And in the day there is a great fire in the sky which ripens the kappa, rouses the animals and gives the light by which men see . . . What is the name of this great fire?''

''It is called the sun.''

''And what is the name of all the land whereon the sun shines?''

''It is called the earth.''

''But the sun does not shine on the earth by night. At night there are many tiny points of light when the sky is clear, but they do not give warmth. What is the Bayani word for these cold, bright points of light?''

''Stars.''

''Shah Shan, I have journeyed among the stars and I swear to you that they seem small and cold only because they are very far away. In reality they are as hot and bright and big as the sun that shines over Baya Nor. Many of them shine on worlds such as this, and their number is greater than all the hairs on all the heads of your people . . . My own home is on a world that is also called Earth. It, too, is warmed by a sun. But it is so far away that a silver bird is needed to make the journey. And now that the silver bird on which I came is dead, I do not think I shall return again.''

Shah Shan was watching him intently. ''There are cities like Baya Nor on your earth?''

"There are cities greater than Baya Nor. Cities where men accomplish wonderful things with metal and other substances."

"Is Oruri worshipped in your cities?"

"For my people, Oruri has many different names."

"And you have god-kings?"

"Yes, but again they are known by different names."

"I have heard," said Shah Shan, smiling, "that Enka Ne permitted you to keep all that was found with you. They were things which the god-king found interesting but of no practical value. Is there anything among these things that would lend weight to the wonders of which you speak?"

Poul Mer Lo hesitated. There was the atomic powered miniature transceiver—the most he could raise on it would be static. There was the electronic wristwatch, a beautiful instrument but lacking, perhaps, the dramatic quality he needed to convince Shah Shan that he spoke the truth.

And there was the sweeper rifle. The ace that he had sworn only to use in extremity.

Should he risk throwing the ace away? He looked at Shah Shan, a boy filled with curiosity and a turmoil of strange new notions. Pour Mer Lo made his decision.

"Stay here," he said. "I will bring you something that is both wonderful and terrible."

He went into the house, took the sweeper rifle from the niche he had made for it and returned to the verandah.

"This," he said, "is a weapon that, if it is used properly could kill half your people."

Shah Shan looked at the small plastic and metal object uncomprehendingly.

"Observe," said Poul Mer Lo. He stood on the verandah, raised the rifle to his shoulder, pushed the breeder button and sighted at the base of a large tree about a hundred metres away. He pressed the trigger.

There was a faint whine, and the rifle vibrated almost imperceptibly. At the base of the tree, a plume of smoke began to rise. Then the tree toppled over.

"Observe," said Poul Mer Lo. He switched his aim to a clear stretch of water on a waterway that was about two hundred metres away. He pressed the trigger. The water began to steam, then boil, then produce a miniature water-spout.

"Observe," said Poul Mer Lo. He aimed at the ground not far from the verandah and blasted a small crater in which the lava hissed and bubbled long after he had put the rifle down.

Shah Shan put out a hand and touched the weapon gingerly. "Truly, it is the work of gods," he said at last. "How many have you destroyed with it?"

Poul Mer Lo smiled. "None. There has been no cause."

"It shall be remembered," said Shah Shan. Then he, too, smiled. "But it did not save you from the darts of the hunters, did it?"

"No, it did not save me from the darts of the hunters."

"That, too, must be remembered," said Shah Shan. He rose. "My lord, you have given me kappa, you have nourished my spirit, you have shown, perhaps, that my friend is not entirely mad. Oruri is our witness . . . I will go now, for time runs swifter than water. And for many there is much thinking to be done. Live in peace, friend of my friend . . . The fingers did not cause too much pain?''

"It is over," said Poul Mer Lo briefly. "It was a small price."

Shah Shan formally touched his lips and his eyes, then turned and went down the verandah steps.

Poul Mer Lo watched him make his way towards the sacred city.

Without speaking, Mylai Tui picked up the empty kappa bowl and the sweeper rifle and took them away.

# NINE

THERE HAD BEEN many discussions aboard the *Gloria Mundi* about the possibility, probability and variety of extra-terrestrial life. During the first three months of the voyage, before any of the twelve crew members had been suspended, the discussions tended to take place on the mess deck after dinner, or in the library. During the last three months of the voyage they tended to take place in the astrodome. But during more than nineteen years of starflight, when only one pair was operational at a time, the favourite place for discussion was the navigation deck. It was there that the ship's log was kept up to date. It was there that diaries were written and letters "posted" for successive pairs so that the month-long vigil would not be too lonely.

It was there that in the seventeenth year of star time, Paul and Ann Marlowe held a champagne and chicken supper to celebrate their successful triumph over the first meteor perforation of the entire voyage. It had not been a very big meteor—less than an inch in diameter—but it had passed with a musical ping clean through the hold of the *Gloria Mundi*, leaving what looked like two neat large calibre bullet holes on each side of the ship's hull.

As soon as the air pressure dropped the alarm bells began to ring. Paul and Ann, mindful of basic training, immediately dashed to the nearest pressure suits and were fully encased long before they were in any danger of explosive decompression. It took them barely five minutes to trace the leaks and another fifteen minutes to process the self-sealer strips and make a chemical weld. Then Paul covered the emergency plugs with two slabs of half-inch titanium, and the crisis was over. It had not been a big crisis really, but it was a good excuse to open one of the bottles of champagne. After he had made a brief statement in the log, Paul scribbled a note to the French pair, who were next on watch. It read: *Since we saved you from a fate worse than freezing, we feel entitled to broach a bottle of the Moet et Chandon '11. I believe it was a very fine year . . . Don't be too envious. We really had to work for it. Paul.*

And so it came about that he and Ann were sitting at table on the navigation deck with the *Moet et Chandon* in a make-shift ice bucket and Altair on the other side of the paraplex window, more than two light years away and looking like a fiery marble.

"Suppose," said Paul, after his second glass, "we came upon a world that was nothing but water. Not a bit of land anywhere. What the hell would we do?"

Ann shook her dark hair and giggled. She had never been much given to alchohol, and the champagne had gone to her head. She hiccupped gravely. "That's easy. Go into low orbit and drop a couple of skin divers complete with aqualungs to look for intelligent sponges."

There was a brief silence. Then Paul said tangentially: "It's an odd thing, but I've never been quite sure whether or not I believe in God."

"What is God?" demanded Ann. "What is God but an extension of the ego—a sort of megalomania by proxy?"

Paul laughed. "Don't mix it with me, dear, in the field of psychological jargon. You're only a gifted amateur. I'm a hardened professional."

"Well, what the hell has God got to do with intelligent sponges?" demanded Ann belligerently.

"Nothing at all . . . Except that if God exists he might just possibly have a sense of humour far more subtle than we bargain for. He might have created intelligent sponges, moronic supermen, parthenogenetic pygmies, immortal sloths or sex-crazed centipedes just for kicks—or just to see what them crazy mixed-up human beings would do when they encountered them."

Ann giggled once more. "If there is a God, and I

don't think there is, I'll bet that human beings are His *pièce de* godlike *résistance*. They are so damn complicated He would have got Himself confused if He'd tried to dream up anything more complicated . . . Anyway, if Altair has inhabitable planets, my money is on sex-crazed centipedes . . . At least it would be amusing. Just think what they could do with all those legs."

Paul filled their champagne glasses again and in doing so emptied the bottle. He gazed at it regretfully. "There are further complications . . . Predestination. Kismet. What if our little venture is not a shot in the dark? What if the whole thing is fully programmed? What if we are all just shoving back the light-years to keep an appointment in Samara."

"You talk a lot of twaddle," said Ann. "Causation is quite nice and cosy—if you don't let it get out of hand. An infinitely variable universe must be filled with infinitely variable possibilities . . . But if you want to know what I think, I think we're going to find no planets at all—or else a stack of bloody burnt out cinders. The one thing we are not going to find is intelligent life."

"Why?"

"Finagle's Second Law."

"And what, pray, is that?"

Ann was incredulous. "You mean to say you've never heard of Finagle's Second Law?"

"I haven't even heard of the first."

Ann hiccupped. "Pardon me. That's the point. There is no first. There is no third, either. Only a second."

"All right, I get the message. I won't even ask

who Finagle was. But what the hell is his Second Law?''

"It states that if in any given circumstances anything can possibly go wrong, it invariably will."

"So you think we'll either score three lemons or come unstuck?"

"It's safer to think that," said Ann darkly. "Nobody in their right mind would tangle with Finagle. The great trick, the ultimate discipline, is always to expect the worst. Then whatever else happens, you're bound to be pleasantly surprised."

Paul was silent for a minute or two. Then he said: "I think I'll go right out on a limb and set myself up as a clairvoyant."

Ann turned to the paraplex window and gazed sombrely at Altair.. "Well, there's your crystal, gypsy mine. What do you see?"

Paul followed her gaze, staring at Altair intently. "I see the jackpot. We shall find an earth-type life-bearing planet. There might even be intelligent beings on it."

"Christ, you're pushing the odds, aren't you?"

"To blazes with the odds," said Paul. "Yes, I'll go all the way. We shall find intelligent beings on it . . . And I rather think we shall keep that appointment in Samara."

Ann smiled. "And what, pray, is that?"

"You mean to say you've never heard of an appointment in Samara?"

"*Touché. Prosit. Grüss Gott* . . . That champagne was terrific."

"It's an oriental tale," said Paul. "And the story goes that the servant of a rich man in Baghdad or

Basra, or some place like that, went out to do a day's shopping. But in the market place he met Death, who gave him a strange sort of look . . . Well the servant chased off home and said to his master: 'Lord, in the market place I met Death, who looked as if he were about to claim me. Lend me your fastest horse that I may ride to Samara, which I can reach before night-fall, and so escape him.' "

"Pretty sensible," said Ann. "Give the servant eight out of ten for initiative."

"Ah," said Paul. "That's the point. The servant displayed too much initiative. The rich man lent the servant his horse, and he duly set off for Samara at a great rate of knots. But when he had gone, the rich man thought: 'This is a bit of a bore. My servant is a jolly good servant. I shall miss him. Death had no right to give him the twitches. I think I'll pop down to the market place and give the old fellow a piece of my mind.' "

"*Noblesse oblige*," said Ann. "A very fine sentiment."

"So the rich man went to the market place and button-holed Death. 'Look here,' he said, or words to that effect, 'what do you mean by giving my servant the shakes?' Death was amused. He said: 'Lord, I merely looked at the fellow in surprise.' 'Why so?' asked the rich man. 'He is just an ordinary servant'. 'I looked at him in surprise,' explained Death, 'because I did not expect to find him here. You see, I have an appointment with him this evening—in Samara.' "

Ann was silent for a while. "Champagne is schizophrenic," she said at length. "One minute it lifts you up, and then it drops you flat on your face

. . . Anyway, we didn't see Death in the market place, did we?"

"Didn't we?" asked Paul. "Didn't we see Death when we went up in orbit? Didn't we see him when we blasted off on the long shot? Don't we make a rude gesture to him every time we pop ourselves back in the cooler?"

"I'm not afraid of dying," said Ann. "I'm only afraid of pain—and of being afraid."

"Poor dear," said Paul. "I'm the spectre at the feast. Dammit, Death just chucked a meteor at us; and it did hardly any damage at all. So he can't be too interested in us, can he?"

"I'm cold," said Ann, "but at the same time just a trifle lascivious. Let's go to bed."

Paul stood up, smiling. "Lasciviousness is all," he said. "Thank God we don't have to keep the house tidy. It's another ten days, I think, before we have to slide ourselves into the freezer."

Ann took his hand. "That's the thought that makes me cold. Meanwhile, come and keep me warm."

There was only one double berth on the *Gloria Mundi*. The crew called it the honeymoon suite. That was where they went.

But even while Paul Marlowe was engaged in the act of love, even as he reached the climax, he was thinking about an appointment in Samara.

There was still the taste of champagne in his mouth, and in Ann's.

But for both of them the taste was sour.

## TEN

HE WOKE UP up and found that he was trembling.
He looked at his surroundings without recognition
for a moment or two, but the disorientation was
brief. Over in the corner of the room a string of
smoke rippled upwards towards the thatch from
the tiny flickering oil lamp set on the miniature
phallus of Oruri. One or two flies buzzed lazily. By
his side, the naked brown girl slept peacefully with
one arm thrown carelessly across his stomach.

He looked at the three stubby fingers and flat-
tened thumb on her small hand. He looked at her
face—neat and serene. An alien face, yet perhaps
it would have raised no eyebrows in central Africa.
Her serenity annoyed him. He shook her into consciousness.

Mylai Tui sat up, bleary-eyed. "What is it, my lord? Surely the nine sisters are still flying?"

"Say it!" he commanded. "Say my name."

"Poul Mer Lo."

He shook her again. "It is not Poul. Say Paul."

"Poul."

"No. Paul."

"Po-el." Mylai Tui enunciated the syllables carefully.

He slapped her. "Po-el," he mimicked. "No, not Po-el. Say Paul."

"Poel."

He slapped her again. "Paul! Paul! Paul! Say it!"

"Pole," sobbed Mylai Tui. "Pole . . . My lord, I am trying very hard."

"Then you are not trying hard enough, Mylai Tui," he snapped brutally. "Why should I bother to speak your language when you can't make a decent sound in mine? Say Paul."

"Pöl."

"That's better . . . Paul."

"Paul."

"That's good. That's very good. Now try Paul Marlowe."

"Pöl Mer Lo."

Again he hit her. "Listen carefully. Paul Marlowe."

"Pöl Mah Lo."

"Paul Marlowe."

"Paul Mah Lo."

"Paul Marlowe."

"Paul . . . Marlowe." By this time Mylai Tui hardly knew what she was saying.

"You've got it!" he exclaimed. "That's it. That's my name. You are to call me Paul. Understand?"

"Yes, my lord."

"Yes, Paul."

"Yes, Paul," repeated Mylai Tui obediently. She wiped the tears from her face.

"It's important, you understand," he babbled. "It's very important. A man has to keep his own name, does he not?"

"Yes, my lord."

He raised his hand.

"Yes, Paul," corrected Mylai Tui hastily. Then she added hesitantly: "My lord is not afflicted by devils?"

He began to laugh. But the laughter disintegrated. And then tears were streaming down his own face. "Yes, Mylai Tui. I am afflicted by devils. It seems that I shall be afflicted by devils as long as I live." Mylai Tui nursed his head on her breast, rocking to and fro, rhythmically. "There is a great sadness inside you," she said at length. "O Paul, my lord, it hisses like water over burning stones. Kill me or send me away; but do not let me witness such pain in one to whom I am not destined to bring the first gift of Oruri."

"What is the first gift of Oruri?"

"A child," said Mylai Tui simply.

He sat up with a jerk. "How do you know that you will not give me a child?"

"Lord—Paul—you have loved me many times."

"Well?"

"I have not worn the zhivo since I left the Temple of Gaiety and gave up the duties of a noia, Paul.

You have loved me many times. If you had been an ordinary Bayani, by now I would have swollen with the fruit of love. I am not swollen. Therefore Oruri withholds his first gift . . . My lord, I have sinned. I know not how, but I have sinned . . . Perhaps you will fare better with another noia.''

He was thunderstruck. For in a terrible moment of clarity he saw that Mylai Tui possessed a wisdom greater then he could ever hope to attain. ''It is true,'' he said calmly. ''I want a child, but I did not know that I want a child . . . There are so many things I do not know . . . Yet, there is no sin, Mylai Tui. For I think that my blood and yours will not mingle. I think that I can never get a child save with one of my own people. And so I shall not send you away.''

Mylai Tui sighed and smiled. ''My lord is merciful. If I cannot bear the son of him who came upon a silver bird, I wish to bear the son of no other.''

He took her hands and looked at her silently for a while. ''What is it that binds us?'' he asked at length.

Mylai Tui could not understand. ''There is nothing to bind us, Paul,'' she said, ''save the purpose of Oruri.''

# ELEVEN

THREE GILDED BARGES, each propelled by eight
pole-men, passed slowly along the Canal of Life
under the great green umbrella of the forest. In the
first barge, guarded by eight brawny priestesses,
there was the small shrouded palanquin that contained the oracle of Baya Nor. In the second barge,
guarded by eight male warriors, was the god-king,
Enka Ne, the council of three and the stranger,
Poul Mer Lo. In the third barge, guarded also by
eight warriors, were the three girl children who
were destined to die.

Poul Mer Lo sat humbly below the dais on which
the god-king reclined, and listened to the words of
his master.

"Life and death," said Enka Ne, in a voice

remarkably like that of Shah Shan, the beggar, "are but two small aspects of the infinite glory of Oruri. Man that is born of woman has but a short time to live, yet Oruri lives both at the beginning of the river of time and at the end. Oruri *is* the river. Oruri is also the people on the river, whose only value is to fulfil his inscrutable purpose. Is this thought not beautiful?"

The bright plumage rustled as Enka Ne took up a more comfortable position. Poul Mer Lo—Paul Marlowe of Earth—found it difficult to believe that, beneath all the iridescent feathers and the imposing bird's head, there was only the flesh and blood of a boy.

"Lord," he said carefully, "whatever men truly believe is beautiful. Worship itself is beautiful, because it gives meaning to the act of living . . . Only pain is ugly, because pain deforms."

Enka Ne gave him a disapproving stare. "Pain is the gift of Oruri. It is the pleasure of Oruri that men shall face pain with gladness and acceptance, knowing that the trial shall bring them closer to the ultimate face . . . See, there is a guyanis! It, too, fulfils the pleasure of Oruri, living for less than a season before it receives the infinite mercy of death."

Poul Mer Lo gazed at the guyanis—a brilliantly coloured butterfly with a wing span longer than his forearm—as it flapped lazily and erratically along the Canal of Life, just ahead of the barge containing the oracle. As he watched, a great bird with leathery wings dived swiftly from a tree-fern on the banks of the canal and struck the guyanis with its toothed beak. One of the butterfly wings sheared completely and drifted down to the surface of the water: the rest of the creature was held firmly in the long black beak. The bird did not even pause in flight.

Enka Ne clapped his hands. "Strike!" he said, pointing to the bird. A warrior raised his blow-pipe to his lips. There was a faint whistle as the dart flew from the pipe. Then the leathery bird, more than twenty metres away, seemed to be transfixed in mid-flight. It hovered for a moment, then spiralled noisily down to the water.

Enka Ne pointed to the warrior who had killed the bird. "Die now," he said gently, "and live for ever."

The man smiled. "Lord," he said, "I am unworthy." Then he took a dart from his pouch and pushed it calmly into his throat. Without another word, he fell from the barge into the Canal of Life.

Enka Ne looked intently at Poul Mer Lo. "Thus is the purpose of Oruri fulfilled."

Poul Mer Lo gazed at the enigmatic waters of the canal. The barge had already left the body of the warrior behind it. Now a butterfly wing floated past and then the still twitching shape of the leathery bird, with the rest of the guyanis still gripped in its beak.

Paul Marlowe, man of Earth, struggled against the dream-like fatalism which had caused him to accept the role of Poul Mer Lo in a dream-like and fatalistic world. But it was hard, because he was still enough of a psychiatrist to realize that two people were inhabiting the same body and were making of it a battleground. Paul would be forever the outcast—technological man, with a headful of sophisticated and synthetic values resisting the stark and simple values of barbarism. Poul was only a man who was trying desparately to belong —a man who wanted nothing more than peace and perhaps a little fulfilment in the world into which he had been thrust.

Was it Paul or was it Poul who was travelling along the Canal of Life with Enka Ne? He did not even know that. He knew only that the great green hypnosis of the forest and the brightly plumed hypnosis of the god-king and the meaning of life and death were all far too much for the would-be fratricides who lived in the same tortured head.

It was a heavy, languorous afternoon. By sunset one of the girl children in the following barge would be sacrificed against the phallus of Oruri in the forest temple of Baya Sur. Poul was fascinated. Paul was shocked. Neither knew what to do.

"Lord," said Paul—or Poul, "which was of greater value: the life of the guyanis or the life of your warrior?"

Enka Ne smiled. "Who can know? No one save Oruri. Was it not Oruri in me that bade the warrior be at one with the guyanis?"

"Who can know?" said the man of Earth. "It is certain that I do not."

The god-king's councillors, crouching together, had heard the exchange in silence. But they were plainly unhappy that a stranger should question the act of Enka Ne. Now one of them spoke.

"Lord," he said diffidently, "may it not be that Poul Mer Lo, whose life is yours, has a careless voice? The affliction may easily be remedied."

Enka Ne shook his feathers and stretched. Then he gazed solemnly at the councillor. "There is no affliction. Know only that the stranger has been touched by Oruri. Whoever would challenge the purpose of Oruri, let him now command the death of Poul Mer Lo."

The councillors subsided, muttering. Poul Mer Lo was sweating with the heat; but somewhere in a dark dimension Paul Marlowe was shivering.

"See," said Enka Ne, "there is the first stone of Baya Sur." He pointed to an obelisk rising from the smooth water of the canal. "Soon there will be a sharp glory. Let no man come to this place without tranquillity and love."

Baya Sur was, unlike Baya Nor, no more than a single stone temple set in the forest and protected from its advance by a high stone wall. At the landing place about forty men—the entire population of Baya Sur, waited to greet the barges. The one containing the oracle was the first to pull in. The palanquin was lifted ashore carefully by the priestesses and carried into the temple. Then Enka Ne gave a signal and his own barge was poled in. He stepped ashore with a great rustling of feathers and with all the arrogance and brightness and mystery of a god. After him came the councillors, and after them came the stranger, Poul Mer Lo. No one stayed to meet the three girl children. Looking over his shoulder as he walked along the paved avenue that led to the temple steps, Poul Mer Lo saw them step ashore and walk gravely after him like tiny clockwork dolls.

Before the sacrifice there was a ritual meal to be

undertaken. It was in the great hall of the phallus where the only source of natural light came from the orifice of a symbolic vagina built into the roof. In the bare walls, however, there were niches; and in the niches were smoky oil lamps.

The palanquin had been set near to the stone phallus. Immediately before the phallus there was a large bowl of kappa and several empty small bowls. The three girl children, silent and immobile, sat cross-legged facing the phallus. Behind them sat three priests, each armed with a short knife. Behind the priests sat the councillors, and behind the councillors sat Poul Mer Lo.

Suddenly, there was a wild desolate bird cry. Enka Ne strutted into the chamber in such a manner that, for a moment, Poul Mer Lo again found it necessary to remind himself that beneath the plumage and under the bright, darting bird's head, there was only a boy. The god-king pecked and scratched. Then he gave his desolate bird cry once more and strutted to the bowl of kappa.

He urinated on it and gave another piercing cry. Then he crouched motionless opposite the palanquin. An answering bird cry came from behind the dark curtains.

One of the priests began to put small handfuls of kappa into the little bowls. The two other priests began to hand the bowls round—first to the girl children, who immediately ate their portions with great relish, then to the councillors, and finally to Poul Mer Lo.

Paul Marlowe wanted to be sick, but Poul Mer Lo forced him to eat. The frugal meal was over in a few moments. Then daylight died, and the room was filled with the flickering shadows cast by the oil lamps.

The god-king rose, strutted to the phallus of Oruri and enfolded it with his wings. Then he whirled and pointed to one of the girl children.

"Come!"

She rose obediently and stepped forward. She turned and leaned back on the phallus, clasping her hands behind it and around it. The god-king suddenly lay at her feet. There was an expression of intense happiness on her face.

One of the priests pressed his arm under her chin, forcing her head back. Another knelt, pressing her stomach so that she was hard against the phallus. The third advanced with knife arm extended and with the other arm ready as if to grasp something.

Enka Ne uttered another bird cry. From the closed palanquin there came an answering bird cry. The knife struck once, then rose and struck again. There was no sound.

The hand plunged into the open chest of the girl and snatched out the still beating heart.

Blood poured from the gaping wound on to the prostrate body of the god-king.

There were two more bird cries—piercing, desolate, triumphant.

Poul Mer Lo fainted.

## TWELVE

THE EXPEDITION, the religious progress, was almost over. So far it had taken eight days and would
be completed on the ninth, when the oracle and
god-king returned to Baya Nor. The three girl children were now safely in the arms of Oruri. The
second had been sacrificed in a manner identical
with that of the first at the temple of Baya Ver and
the third at the temple of Baya Lys.

Poul Mer Lo had learned not to faint at the
spectacle of a living heart being torn from the body
of a child. It was, he had been told, at the best
rather impolite. At the worst it could be construed
as an unfavourable omen.

Now, on the eighth night shortly after the ceremonial death-in-life feast that followed the sac-

rifice, he lay restlessly on his bed in one of the guest cells of Baya Lys. He was wondering why Enka Ne had invited/commanded his presence on the journey. To accompany the oracle and the god-king on a religious progress was a privilege normally reserved only for those who had distinguished themselves greatly in war or worship.

Suddenly he became aware that someone else was in the cell. He sat up quickly and saw by the light of the small oil lamp a half-starved youth in a tattered samu squatting patiently on the floor. There was a covered bundle by his side.

"Oruri greets you," said Shah Shan, rising.

"The greeting is a blessing," answered Poul Mer Lo mechanically.

"I sorrow if I have disturbed your meditations."

Poul Mer Lo smiled. "My meditations were such that I welcome one who interrupts them."

Shah Shan indicated the bundle at his feet. "My friend, of whom I think you know, bade me bring you some things that were found in the forest. He was of the opinion that they would have some meaning for you." He untied the piece of cloth and displayed the contents of the bundle.

There was one plastic visor, two atomic grenades and a battered transceiver.

Poul Mer Lo was instantly transformed into Paul Marlowe who, gazing at the odd collection, felt a stinging mistiness in his eyes.

"Who found these things?" he managed to say at last.

"The priests of Baya Lys."

They have found nothing else?"

"Nothing . . . Except . . ." Shah Shan hesitated.

"My friend told me that it has been reported that a great blackened hole exists in the forest where formerly there was nothing but trees and grass. These objects are certainly very curious. Do they have any significance?"

"They belonged to those who travelled with me in the silver bird." Paul Marlowe picked up one of the atomic grenades. "This, for example, is a terrible weapon of destruction. If I were to move these studs in a certain way," he indicated two tiny recessed levers, "the whole of Baya Lys would be consumed by fire."

Shah Shan was imperturbed. "It is to be hoped," he remarked, "that, receiving the guidance of Oruri, you will not cause this thing to happen."

Paul smiled. "Be assured that I will not cause it to happen, Shah Shan, for it would encompass my own death also."

The boy was silent for a while. "The domain of Baya Nor is bounded by one day's march to the north," he said at last. "Beyond that is land occupied by a barbaric people. It may be that your friends have become the friends of these people . . . Or they may have been killed, or they may have wandered and died in the forest . . . How many travelled with you?"

"There were twelve of us altogether."

"And three came to Baya Nor."

"Three were taken prisoner by the people of Baya Nor."

The boy shrugged. "It matters not how we describe the event. Nine still remain shrouded by mystery."

"These people of the forest—how are they called?"

"They call themselves the Lokh. We call them Lokhali. They speak a strange tongue."

"It is possible to meet and talk with the Lokhali?"

Shah Shan smiled. "Possible, but not advisable. And it is likely that the conversation would be brief. These people live for war."

"Perhaps if Enka Ne were to send presents, and ask for news . . ."

Shah Shan stiffened. "Enka Ne does not treat with the Lokhali. So it has always been. So it will always be. Doubtless in the end Oruri will grant them a terrible affliction . . . Poul Mer Lo, my friend is puzzled. The oracle has pronounced that you are a great teacher and that because of you greatness shall be bestowed upon Baya Nor."

"I do now know that I am a great teacher. So far my teaching has been very small."

"Then, my lord, you must make it big," said Shah Shan simply, "for the oracle speaks only the truth . . . My friend is rich in glory but not rich in time. He wishes to see the fruits of your teaching before he answers the call."

"Shah Shan, your friend must not expect too much. The essence of teaching is to learn first and then teach afterwards."

"Permit me to observe, Poul Mer Lo, that the essence of teaching is to be understood . . . It was many days before you learned to speak Bayani, was it not?"

"Many days indeed."

"What, then, is the tongue you would speak with your own kind?"

"It is called English."

"I wish to speak this Ong Lys. For then I might more perfectly understand the thoughts of Poul Mer Lo."

"Shah Shan, what is the use? There is no one but I who can speak this tongue."

"Perhaps, my lord, that is why I wish to learn it . . . I am a poor and insignificant person, having nothing to offer you. But my friend would be greatly pleased."

Paul Marlowe smiled. "It shall be as you wish, Shah Shan. Your friend is either very clever or very simple."

Shah Shan looked at him in surprise. "You do not know which?" he asked. "But why cannot my friend be both?"

# THIRTEEN

PAUL MARLOWE banged the calabash hard against the step of the verandah where he was sitting. Silently, Mylai Tui poured some more kappa spirit into it.

He took a long swig and felt a bitter satisfaction as the fiery liquid wrought havoc in his throat and his stomach. He was getting drunk rapidly and he didn't give a damn.

"Big breasted brown-faced bitch," he muttered in English.

"My lord?" said Mylai Tui uncertainly.

"Say Paul, damn you!" Again in English.

"Paul?" repeated Mylai Tui anxiously. It was the only word she had caught.

"Thank you," he snapped in Bayani. "Now be silent. There are times when a man needs to become a fool. This is one of them."

Mylai Tui bowed her head and sat cross-legged, cradling the pitcher of kappa spirit in her lap, mindful of the future needs of Poul Mer Lo.

It was twilight and the nine moons of Altair Five were pursuing each other across the sky like . . . Like what? thought Paul Marlowe . . . Like frightened birds . . . Nine cosmic cinders on the wing . . .

"I am dead," he said in English. "I am a corpse with a memory . . . What the hell is going on in Piccadilly Circus tonight? Who won the test match, and what sensational scandals will break in the Sunday papers tomorrow? For clearly tonight is Saturday night. Therefore let there be a great rejoicing."

He emptied the calabash, shuddered, and banged it against the verandah step once more. Silently, Mylai Tui refilled it.

He wanted to listen to Beethoven—any old Beethoven would do. But the nearest stereo was a fair number of light years away. Damn!

"I shall declaim," said Paul Marlowe to no one in particular. "Is there not reason to declaim? It was in another country, and, besides, the wench is dead."

"Paul?" said Mylai Tui uncertainly.

"Shut up! Jew of Malta—I think—by kind permission of a bleeding ancestor."

"Paul?"

"Shut up, or I will gorily garotte you, you brown-bottomed whore." He began to laugh at the alliteration, but the laughter degenerated into a fit of coughing. He cleared his throat.

*"Only speaking in the tongues of men,"* he said.
*"What can I make of a broken image,*
*a single shaft of light,*
*a white star over winter marshes*
*when harsh cries of night birds*
*quiver above unheard voices, and the river*
*sings like a whip of laughter in the misty twilight?"*

"Paul?" said Mylai Tui again, with great temerity.

"Be silent, you bloody ignorant female beast! I speak the words of some goddammed twentieth-century poet whose name temporarily escapes me . . . Why do I speak the words of said anon poet? I will tell you, you little Bayani slut. Because there is a hole inside me. A hole, do you hear? A damn big hole, one heart wide and twenty light-years deep . . . I am dead, Horatio . . . Where the hell is the rest of that rot-gut?"

Mylai Tui said nothing. If it pleased her lord to speak with the voice of the devil, obviously there was nothing to be said. Or done.

"Where the hell is the rest of that rot-gut?" demanded Paul Marlowe, still in English.

Mylai Tui did not move.

He stood up, lurched forwards unsteadily and kicked the pitcher out of her hands. The kappa spirit was spilled all over the verandah. Its sweet smell rose suffocatingly.

Paul Marlowe fell flat on his face and was sick.

Presently, when she had cleaned him up, Mylai Tui managed to drag him inside the house. She tried to lift him up to the bed but was not strong enough.

He lay snoring heavily on the floor.

# FOURTEEN

THE DIABOLICAL machine was finished. It stood outside the small thatched house that was the home of Poul Mer Lo. The two workmen, one a woodcutter and the other a mason, who had built it under the direction of the stranger, stood regarding their achievement, grinning and gibbering like a pair of happy apes. Poul Mer Lo had hired them for the task at a cost of one copper ring each. According to Mylai Tui, it was gross overpayment; but he felt that munificence—if, indeed, it was munificence—was appropriate. It was not often that a man was granted the privilege of devizing something that would change the pattern of an entire civilization.

Mylai Tui squatted on the verandah and regarded the machine impassively. She neither understood nor cared that, in the world of Baya Nor,
she had just witnessed a technological revolution.
If the building of the contraption had given Poul
Mer Lo some pleasure, then she was glad for his
sake. Nevertheless, she was a little disappointed
that a man who was clearly destined for greatness
and whose thanu had raised her to ecstasy should
dissipate his spirit in the construction of useless
toys.

"What do you think of it?" asked Poul Mer Lo.

Mylai Tui smiled. "It is ingenious, my lord. Who
knows, perhaps it is also beautiful. I am not skilled
to judge the purpose of this thing it has pleased my
lord to create."

"My name is Paul."

"Yes, Paul. I am sorry. It is only that it gives me
some happiness to call you my lord."

"Then you must remember, Mylai Tui, that it
also gives me some happiness to hear you call me
Paul."

"Yes, Paul. This I know, and this I must remember."

"Do you know what you are looking at?"

"No, Paul."

"You are looking at something for which there is
no Bayani word. So I must give you a word from
my own tongue. This thing is called a cart."

"A kay-urt."

"No. A cart."

"A kayrt."

"That is better. Try it again—cart."

"Kayrt."

"This cart runs on wheels. Do you know what wheels are?"

"No, Paul."

"Say the word—wheels."

"Wells."

"That is good. Wheels, Mylai Tui, are what men need to lift the burden from their backs."

"Yes, Paul."

"You have seen the poor people hauling logs, carrying water and bending themselves double under heavy loads of kappa and meat."

"Yes, Paul."

"The cart," said Poul Mer Lo, "will make all this toil no longer necessary. With the cart, one man will be able to carry the burden of many, and because of this many men will be free to do more useful work. Is that not a wonderful thought?"

"Truly, it is a wonderful thought," responded Mylai Tui obediently.

"Lord," said one of the workmen, "now that we have built the kayrt, what is your pleasure?"

"It is my pleasure to visit Enka Ne," said Poul Mer Lo. "It is my pleasure to take this gift to the god-king, that in his wisdom, he will cause many carts to be built, thus greatly easing the toil of the people of Baya Nor."

Suddenly the smile vanished from the face of the small Bayani. "Lord, to build the kayrt is one thing—indeed, it has given much amusement—but to deliver it to Enka Ne is another."

"You are afraid?"

"It is proper to be afraid, my lord. It is proper to fear the glory of Enka Ne."

"It is proper, also," said Poul Mer Lo, "to make

offerings to the god-king. I am a stranger in this land, and the cart is my offering. Come, let us go . . . See, I shall ride in the cart and you, taking the shafts, shall draw me. It may be that Enka Ne will have need of men who know how to fit a wheel to an axle. Come.''

Poul Mer Lo perched himself on top of the small cart and waited patiently. The two Bayani muttered briefly to each other and urinated where they stood. He had witnessed such a ritual many times. It was the way in which a low-caste Bayani anticipated sin by giving himself absolution beforehand.

Presently, having touched hands and shoulders, the two men took a shaft each and began to draw the cart slowly along the Road of Travail towards the Third Avenue of the Gods. Poul Mer Lo waved cheerily to Mylai Tui.

''Oruri be with you,'' she called, ''at the end as at the beginning.''

''Oruri be with you always,'' responded Poul Mer Lo. Then he added informally: ''Let there be the paint of dancing upon you this night. Then shall pleasure visit us both.''

It was a fine morning. The air was clear and warm but not heavy. As Poul Mer Lo sat on his cart, listening to the squeaky protest of the wooden wheels against the stone axle-tree, he felt at peace with the world.

A light wind was blowing in from the forest. It carried scents that were still strange and intoxicating to him. It carried the incense of mystery, the subtle amalgam of smells that made him feel almost at times that he was the most fortunate man in the universe. Here, indeed, was the farther shore. And his footprints were upon it.

Presently, the cart overtook a group of early morning hunters returning to the city, laden with their kill. They gazed at the vehicle in amazement. Poul Mer Lo smiled at them gaily.

"Oruri greets you," he said.

"The greeting is a blessing," they returned.

"Lord," said one, "what is the thing upon which you sit and which men may move so easily?"

"It is a cart. It runs on wheels. With the grace of Enka Ne, soon you will be carrying your meat to Baya Nor on carts. Soon the people of Baya Nor will learn to ride on wheels."

"Lord," said the hunter, perplexed, "truly it is a wondrous thing. I pray only that it may be blessed by a sign."

"What sign?"

"Lord, there is only the sign of Oruri."

"The cart had now reached the end of the Road of Travail, and the broad dirt track gave way to the broader and stone paved Third Avenue of the Gods. The wheels rattled noisily over the cobbestones. There were more people about—city people, sophisticated Bayani, both high and low born, who gazed at Poul Mer Lo with a mixture of what he interpreted as amusement and awe.

He would have been more accurate if he had interpreted the smiling stares as antagonism and awe. But he was not aware of the antagonism until it was too late.

The cart was already half across the causeway leading to the sacred city. By this time it had collected a retinue of more than fifty Bayani. This, in itself, was not unfortunate.

What was unfortunate was that Poul Mer Lo should encounter one of the blind black priests and that the wheels of the cart should pass over his bare toes.

The priest screamed and tore the hood from his face.

His eyes, unaccustomed to daylight, were screwed up painfully for quite a long time before he was able to focus on Poul Mer Lo.

"Oruri will destroy!" he shouted in a loud voice. "This thing is an affliction to the chosen. Oruri will destroy!"

There was a dreadful silence. Poul Mer Lo gazed at the hoodless priest uncomprehendingly.

Then somebody threw the first stone. It bounced off the cart harmlessly. But it was a signal.

More stones came. The crowd began to rumble. Part of the causeway itself was torn up as ammunition.

"Oruri speaks!" screamed the priest.

And then the stones began to fall like giant hail.

"Stop!" shouted Poul Mer Lo. "Stop! The cart is a gift for Enka Ne."

But the woodcutter, holding one of the shafts, had already been struck in the small of the back by a sharp piece of rock. He fell, bleeding. The mason abandoned his shaft and tried to flee. The crowd seized him.

"Stop!" shouted Poul Mer Lo. "In the name of Enka Ne, I—"

He never finished the sentence. A strangely

heavy round pebble, expertly aimed by a child on the fringe of the crowd, caught him on the forehead. He went down with the sound of a great roaring in his ears.

## FIFTEEN

POUL MER LO was aware of an intense, throbbing pain. He opened his eyes. He was in a room to which there seemed to be no windows. Here and there, smoky oil lamps burned in niches in the stone walls.

He felt cold.

He tried to move, and could not.

He was chained to a stone slab.

A Bayani with a white hood over his face leaned over the slab and peered through narrow eye-slits. "The spirit has returned," he announced to someone outside Poul Mer Lo's field of vision. "Now the stranger will speak."

"Who—who are you? What am I doing here? What happened?"

"I am Indrui Sa, general of the Order of the Blind Ones. You are Poul Mer Lo, a stranger in this land, quite possibly an instrument of chaos."

"Where are the two men who were with me?"

"Dead."

"What happened to them?"

"Oruri crushed them to his bosom. Stranger, they were the victims of chaos. Speak of them no more. Their names are undone. Their fathers had no sons. Their sons had no fathers. They are without meaning . . . But you, stranger, you Oruri did not take. Oruri looked upon you but he did not take you. This we must understand."

"I was going to Enka Ne in the sacred city. I was taking him the cart I had caused to be built."

"Enka Ne had called you?"

"No," answered Poul Mer Lo.

"Help him," said the Bayani in the hood.

From out of the gloom another dark shape advanced.

Poul Mer Lo felt the sudden touch of cold metal on his stomach. Then he screamed.

He gazed, horrified, at the pincers gripping a large fold of his flesh.

"I grieve for you," said Indrui Sa. "The god-king receives only those who are called . . . Help him!"

The pincers were tightened and twisted. Poul Mer Lo screamed again.

"Thus, perhaps, Oruri hears your sorrow," said Indrui Sa. "It may be that your ignorance and presumption will inspire some mercy . . . Stranger, you rode not upon an animal but upon that which had been built by the hand of man. How call you this thing?"

"It is a cart."

"Help him!"

Again the pincers were tightened and twisted. Again Poul Mer Lo screamed.

"The kayrt is no more. Oruri saw fit to destroy it. What did you hope to encompass with this kayrt?"

"It was a gift," sobbed Poul Mer Lo. "It was a gift to Enka Ne. I thought—I thought that if the god-king saw the use to which the cart could be put, he would cause many of them to be built. Thus would the toil of men be greatly eased."

"Stranger," said Indrui Sa, "human toil is the gift of Oruri. Let no man diminish that gift . . . Help him."

Once more the pincers tightened and twisted. Poul Mer Lo screamed and fainted. When he became conscious once more, Indrui Sa was still speaking. He sounded as if he had been speaking a long time.

"And therefore," said Indrui Sa, "it is clear, is it not, that you were the uncomprehending instrument of chaos. Two men have been destroyed, the kayrt has been destroyed and the foot of the priest will require much rest. Repent, Poul Mer Lo, of ignorance. Repent also of presumption. Give thanks to Oruri for the blessing of a speedy death which, bearing in mind the degree of chaos you have already inspired is more than—"

Suddenly there was a wild desolate bird cry.

Instantly Indrui Sa stopped speaking and fell upon his face.

Poul Mer Lo heard a rustling and saw a bright, darting bird's head and brilliant plumage that glistened even in the lamplight.

"Who speaks of death?" asked a high, reedy voice.

There was silence.

The god-king gave his piercing cry once more. "Who speaks of death?"

Indrui Sa picked himself up. "Lord, the stranger brings chaos."

But who speaks of death?"

"Lord, chaos is the product of unbeing, therefore unbeing is the reward of chaos."

"Oruri hears you, Indrui Sa, most worthy of men and upholder of the law. Oruri hears you and is desirous of your company."

Indrui Sa stiffened and remained motionless.

Paul Mer Lo was vaguely aware of others coming into the chamber.

Enka Ne uttered his bird cry once more. "Strike!" he said.

A warrior stepped forward and thrust a short trident into the throat of Indrui Sa. There was a brief whistling noise, then he fell suddenly.

"Release the instrument of chaos," commanded Enka Ne. Then, without waiting to see if his command was carried out, he turned and left the chamber.

Presently, Poul Mer Lo found himself stumbling up a narrow spiral staircase, stumbling out into the brilliant and painful sunlight.

# SIXTEEN

"IT IS VERY strange," said Shah Shan, speaking excellent English, "this friendship that exists between us. We are men of two worlds, Paul. It is strange that Oruri should guide you across the great darkness of space to shed some light in the darkness of my mind." He laughed. "One is tempted to look for a pattern."

"Shah Shan, you have a great talent for learning," said Paul Marlowe. "In two hundred days—four Bayani months—you have learned to speak my language better than many people in my own world who have studied it for years."

"That is because I wish to see into your thoughts."

"On Earth, we should undoubtedly call you a genius."

Shah Shan laughed. "I do not think so. From what you have told me, your planet has many who are more gifted than I."

"By our reckoning," said Paul, "you are nineteen years old—still a boy. Yet you rule a kingdom wisely, and you have assimilated more information in a few months than our most talented young men can assimilate in as many years."

Shah Shan shrugged. "Please, Paul, humour me a little. For me the old ways of thinking die hard. Enka Ne rules Baya Nor. Shah Shan is merely his shadow, a simple waterman."

Paul laughed. "Ritual schizophrenia."

"I beg your pardon?"

"I'm sorry. I meant that in a sense you have two excellent minds, both able to perfectly control the same body."

"Oruri speaks for Enka Ne," retorted Shah Shan. Then he grinned. "But Shah Shan is insignificant enough to speak for himself."

"Paul," said Mylai Tui in English with an atrocious accent, "will you dronk some mare kappa spreet?"

"Ask our guest first, love."

"I am sorry, Shah Shan, police you will dronk?"

Shah Shan held out his calabash. "Police I will dronk," he said gravely.

The three of them were taking their ease on the verandah of Paul's little house. It had been a hot day, but though the evening was still warm, the clouded skies had rolled away to reveal a fine, far dusting of stars. Overhead the nine small moons of

Altair Five flew raggedly westward like bright migrating birds.

Paul Marlowe looked at the moons and the stars without seeing either. He was thinking of the last few months, of the time since Shah Shan had begun to come to him regularly to learn English. He knew that it was difficult for Enka Ne to make time for Shah Shan, and he had been puzzled as to why the boy should devote so much precious energy and concentration to learning a language he could only ever hope to speak with one person.

But then he realized that Shah Shan was not so much intent upon learning a language as upon learning all he could of the world that existed on the other side of the sky. Instinctively, the boy knew that the Bayani language was inadequate, that its simple collection of nouns and verbs and qualifying words could only provide a horribly distorted picture of the world that had once belonged to Paul Marlowe.

So Shah Shan, with the typical fanaticism of genius, had applied himself not only to a new language but to the attitudes and philosophy of the one man who spoke that language. He had used Paul like an encyclopaedia; and in four Bayani months he had mastered not only the language but much of the knowledge of the man who spoke it.

"You know, of course," said Shah Shan, "that in twenty-three days Enka Ne will return to the bosom of Oruri?"

Paul sighed. "Yes, I know. But—is it necessary?"

"So it has always been. The god-king reigns for

a year. Then Oruri sees fit to renew the form."

"But is it necessary?"

Shah Shan regarded him calmly. And in the eyes of the boy there seemed to Paul Marlowe to be a wisdom that passed beyond the realm of understanding.

"It is necessary," said Shah Shan softly. "The face of a civilization cannot be changed in a single lifetime, Paul. You should know that. If Enka Ne did not offer himself gladly and with great joy, Baya Nor would disintegrate. Factions would arise. Most probably the end would be civil war . . . No. Enlightenment must come slowly, peacefully. You, the instrument of chaos, are also the instrument of progress. You must plant the seed and hope that others will reap the harvest."

"Shah Shan, you are the first man to bring tears to my eyes."

"Let us hope that I am also the last. I know nothing of the new god-king. He has been found already, and is being instructed. But I know nothing of him. It may be that he will be more— what is the word I want?"

"Orthodox?" suggested Paul.

"Yes, more orthodox. Perhaps he will insist on tradition. You will have to be careful. "Shah Shan laughed. "Remember what happened when you introduced us to the wheel?"

"Three men died," said Paul. "But now your citizens are able to use carts, wheelbarrows, rickshaws."

Shah Shan took a deep draught of the kappa spirit. "No, Paul, your arithmetic is wrong. I have not told you this before, but Enka Ne was forced to execute one hundred and seventeen priests—mostly of the blind order—in order to preserve your life and to permit the building of carts. It was a high price, was it not?''

Paul Marlowe looked at him, appalled.

# SEVENTEEN

IT WAS A grey, cool morning. Winds blew erratically and disturbingly from the forest, filling the city of Baya Nor with strange odours—musky intimations of mortality.

Death had been very much on the mind of Paul Marlowe. It was the prospect of death—and, perhaps, the recent spate of English lessons—that had caused a reversion to type. Poul Mer Lo, the pseudo Bayani, had given way to Paul Marlowe, an Englishman of the twenty-first century of Earth. A man who was depressed and revolted by the fact that his only friend on this alien world would be joyfully going to his death in six more days.

He had grown to love Shah Shan. Love on Earth reflected Paul bitterly, was suspect if not obsolete.

And love for a man was more than obsolete: it was perverted. But here on this other fragment of dust on the other side of the sky, love could be admitted. There need be no justifications, no feelings of guilt, no sense of shame.

But why did he love Shah Shan? Was it because, as Enka Ne, the boy had spared his life when it would have been so much safer, so much easier to have given thumbs down? Was it because, back on that other burnt out particle of fire, he Paul, had never had a brother? Or a son . . .

No matter what the reason, the fact remained. Shah Shan was going to die. Or, rather, Enka Ne, the god-king was drawing close to the bosom of Oruri. And the brightest mind in the whole of Baya Nor was going to be sacrificed to the senseless traditions and superstitions of an ignorant little tribe that had not changed its way for hundreds of years.

What was that Bayani proverb? He who is alive cannot die. Paul Marlowe laughed. God damn Oruri! Then he laughed again as he realized that he had only called on one god to confound another.

Because of his sadness he had wanted solitude. So he had left the small house and Mylai Tui and had wandered slowly along the bank of the Canal of Life until he came to where the kappa fields met the heavy green perimeter of the forest. And now he was sitting on a small mound, watching the women toiling in the muddy fields as they tended the new crop.

They were singing. The words came to him faintly, intermittently across the indecisive gusts of wind . . .

*"A little kappa, a little love.*
*Oruri listens, waiting above.*
*A little kappa, a little light.*
*Oruri brings the gift of night.*
*A little kappa, a little song.*
*The day is short, the night is long."*

Yes, though Paul savagely, God damn Oruri! Oruri was the millstone round these people's necks, the concept that kept them in a static, medieval society with a medieval technology and medieval attitudes that would hold them back for a thousand years.

God damn Oruri!

Suddenly, his silent monologue, his reverie of exasperation was broken by a long-drawn high pitched cry. He had never heard such a cry before. He didn't know whether it was animal or human, whether it was close or distant.

The cry came again, this time ending in a gasp. It was close—so close that he was briefly tempted to believe he had made it himself.

It came from somewhere on the other side of the mound.

He scrambled the few steps to the top of the hillock and looked down. There at the base on the other side a small Bayani woman squatted over a hole in the ground. It looked as if she had scooped the hole out of the rich soft soil with her fingers, for it was arranged in two neat piles on each side of her; and her hands were buried in the fresh, moist earth—presumably supporting her as she squatted.

She had not seen him. Her gaze was fixed directly on the ground ahead of her. As he watched, fascinated, the cry came once more.

It was not a cry of pain, nor was it a cry of fear. For no reason at all, the word keening came into Paul's mind. He had never heard real primitive keening; but this, he supposed, was how it must sound.

Oddly, he felt that he was intruding upon something intensely private. Yet, consumed with curiosity, he wanted to stay and watch. He lay down on the top of the mound, trying to make himself as inconspicuous as possible. For a moment, the woman stretched, raising her head to the sky and sweeping the long hair from her face with a soil-stained hand. Then she fell back into the squatting position and let out another weird cry.

He saw that she was big with child.

And he understood that, for reasons best known to herself, she had come to this desolate spot to give birth.

He witnessed the entire operation. It did not take long. The woman began to pant and bear down rhythmically. Soon the crown of the baby's head had been forced past the lips of the vagina. Presently, its tiny body slid like a small dark fish into the hole that had been prepared for it.

The woman rested for a time—still in the squatting position. Then with a movement that could not have been emulated by any European woman, and probably not by any woman of Earth, she bent expertly down, her head and shoulders low between her knees, and bit through the umbilical cord.

Having done that, she knotted the length that

was still attached to the baby's stomach and then lifted the tiny body out of the hole, resting it on one of the piles of soft earth, where it began to cry lustily. It was not long, then, before the afterbirth came. The woman uttered one more cry—softer this time—then stood up and stretched herself. The wind from the forest blew, catching her long hair and streaming it behind her. She looked for a moment like a small black statue, cut from living rock, courageously defying time and the elements.

Then the moment was gone for ever as, with a matter of fact gesture, she scooped up the new-born baby and with her feet swept the soil back into the hole on top of the steaming afterbirth. When the operation was finished, and still clutching the baby possessively to her breast, she stamped the earth flat. Then she sat down cross-legged to examine the child to whom she had just given birth.

Paul Marlowe stared at her, obsessed with the notion that the entire incident was all part of some bizarre dream.

Suddenly, she began to keen once more. This time the sound was shrill and desolate. It was a cry from the soul, a cry of anguish. And he knew that the dream was real.

He stood up. The woman saw him. The sound died in her throat. She held the baby to her apprehensively, almost as if she were trying to deny its existence. For the first time there was fear on her face.

Paul scrambled down the hillock.

"Oruri greets you," he said gently.

"The greeting is a blessing," she murmured.

But there was a sob in her voice that she did not manage wholly to stifle.

"Forgive me, but I was on the other side of the hill. I heard you and came to see what was happening. I could not help but watch."

"Lord, there is nothing to forgive." The tears were streaming down her face. "Truly, lord, there is nothing to forgive—except that . . ." she could restrain herself no longer. Sobbing shook her small body; and the child at her breast became silent in the presence, perhaps, of tragedy.

"What is it, my daughter?" Unconsciously Paul lapsed into the vernacular Bayani.

"O, my father, this, before Oruri—for whom I have nothing but love—is my third mortal sin. I weep because the blade of Enka Ne must now pass through my womb and through the fruit of my womb. Unless . . . Unless . . ."

Paul Marlowe was perplexed. "Unless what?"

"Unless my father is graciously able to unsee what he has now seen. Unless the greater purpose of Oruri can only be fulfilled by the departure of myself and this poor fragment of my flesh."

"My daughter, what is wrong? The child lives and you live. Can more be asked?"

The woman had recovered herself a little. "Yes, lord," she said defiantly, "more can be asked. Much more can be asked. Observe the third sin." She held out the child.

Paul Marlowe stared at it uncomprehendingly.

"My daughter, you have a fine, strong son. Worse may happen in life than to bear such a child."

"Observe!" said the woman, almost as a command. She held out the baby's left hand.

Paul Marlowe noted the three tiny fingers and thumb closing and unclosing spasmodically. Instantly, he felt a slight discomfort and prickling where the small finger had been struck from each of his hands by the orders of Enka Ne a few months ago.

"So, your child is vigorous, my daughter," he managed to say.

"Observe!" repeated the woman, dully. She held out the baby's right hand. On this one, *four* fingers and a thumb opened and closed spasmodically.

Paul Marlowe was dumbfounded. Four fingers and a thumb!

"Now my father will understand why I must go from this place and not display myself or this mortal sin in Baya Nor."

He gazed at her blankly.

Suddenly, she fell to her knees and pressed her head against his legs. "My lord, you are a stranger and therefore, perhaps, Oruri has granted you a greater wisdom. Say only that you will unsee what you have seen. Say only that I may go peacefully from this place. I do not ask more."

"My daughter, there is much that I do not understand."

"Lord, there is much that none understands— save Oruri and Enka Ne. Say only that I may go from this place. Say only that you will unsee what you have seen." She gripped him painfully, beseechingly. He could feel the salt tears from her eyes upon his flesh.

"From me, there is nothing for you to fear," he

said softly. "Truly, I will unsee what I have seen
. . . But, my daughter, where will you go?"

She pointed to the dark green rim of the forest.
"There, my father, is no sin and no punishment. It
is where I and my child will live or die."

"I hope, then, that you will live," he managed to
say.

The woman rose to her feet, and smiled. "Pray
for me," she said simply. "I have much need of
it." She turned away.

As in a trance, Paul Marlowe watched her walk
purposefully towards the line of trees and shrubs
that swayed in the cool breeze like an emerald sea.

Faintly, the voices of the singers in the kappa
fields came to him: *The day is short, the night is
long.*

# EIGHTEEN

AFTER A LONG day spent in stretching and drying the largest kappa leaves he could find, until they became tough and durable like parchment, Paul Marlowe—feeling oddly, now, more like Poul Mer Lo—occupied his favourite position on the verandah step of his small thatched house. Inside the house, Mylai Tui was cooling kappa spirit by patiently dipping the earthenware jar in a large pitcher of water and allowing the water on the jar to evaporate. Presently, she would bring him a brimming calabash. Presently, he would get drunk.

It was seventeen days since Enka Ne the 609th had returned to the bosom of Oruri. As the sun swung low on the western horizon, Paul Marlowe allowed his gaze to drift across the serene stretch of water that was called the Mirror of Oruri towards the sacred city and the lofty Temple of the Weeping Sun.

He had not been present at the ceremony. Only those of high rank were permitted to be present on such solemn occasions. But Shah Shan had described the ritual to him on his last visit, three days before the event. It was attended, apparently, with all the pomp and ceremony of an ancient terrestrial coronation—with horrific variations.

A coronation in reverse. For as Enka Ne approached the stone phallus against which he would lean joyfully while the living heart was torn from his chest, he would be stripped of all his regalia until nothing remained to be despatched to the bosom of Oruri but Shah Shan, a Bayani waterman with a fine brain and an excellent command of English.

As soon as the blow had been struck and the beating heart removed—to the accompaniment of a great cry of joy from all present—the body would be allowed to fall to the base of the phallus. And then there would be the answering call—a single desolate bird cry; and Enka Ne the 610th would strut from behind the phallus, a bird covered in brilliant plumage, with iridescent feathers of blue and red and green and gold, and with brilliant yellow eyes and a hooked black beak.

The king is dead. Long live the king!

Thus would the enduring glory of Oruri have been reaffirmed.

Paul Marlowe gazed across the water at the Temple of the Weeping Sun. And tears ran down his cheeks, unheeded.

Mylai Tui brought the calabash, full of cooled spirit.

"Thank you, my love," said Paul in English.

"Think nothing of it," said Mylai Tui dutifully. It was a phrase she had learned most carefully. She sat patiently, waiting for the further commands of her lord.

Paul took a deep draught of the kappa spirit. Fire coursed through his veins. But his head remained cool and empty.

He was thinking of what Shah Shan had said to him at their last meeting.

"You must not be sad, Paul," he had said. "You do not yet understand the ways of my people. But you must not be sad. It may be that Enka Ne will think of you when he is called. It may be that he will wish to send you some small token for the kindness and patience you have shown to an insignificant waterman."

Sure enough, on the day of the sacrifice, a black Bayani of the god-king's personal guard had brought him one hundred and twenty-eight copper rings and one long green feather from the plumage of Enka Ne. Paul had been about to ask him if Enka Ne had sent any message, when the great cry of sacrifice drifted across the water from the Temple of the Weeping Sun. A look of intense happiness had come over the face of the small Bayani warrior. Without a word, he had reversed his short trident and, with a tremendous thrust, plunged it into his own throat. The death was spectacular and messy, but it was also almost instantaneous.

Paul Marlowe took another drink from the calabash and gazed at Mylai Tui.

"Do you remember a bright lad by the name of Shah Shan," he said in English thickly, "a youngster whose eyes were full of fire and whose brain was full of nine million nine hundred and ninety-nine thousand question marks?"

"I do not understand, lord," answered Mylai Tui in Bayani. She was accustomed to his increasing use of the strange tongue, but rarely accustomed to his meaning.

"Say Paul, blast you."

"I am sorry, Paul," she said in English. "You speak too quickly."

He switched to Bayani. "Do you remember Shah Shan—the first time he came to this house?"

"Yes, lord," she answered in Bayani. "I remember the first visit of Shah Shan. He was very thin, very hungry."

Paul took another drink. "He had bright, searching eyes. He had the gift of greatness . . . I am sad that he will come no more."

"Lord," said Mylai Tui simply, "I rejoice, having seen the visage of a god upon the face of a man."

"The god is now dead," said Paul grimly.

"No, lord, the man is now dead. The god lives. So it has always been. So it will always be."

"World without end," he mocked, raising the calabash to his lips. For some time, now, his relationship with Mylai Tui had been strained. Thinking back, he decided that it had begun to show signs of strain when Shah Shan started to come regularly for his English lessons. Until that time Paul Marlowe, native of Earth had done his best—despite lapses—to become Poul Mer Lo of

Baya Nor. He had been very reliant on Mylai Tui and had tried to draw close to her and understand her way of looking at things.

But then Shah Shan with his quick mind and natural curiosity had met him on his own ground and, learning not only the language but the ways of the land on the other side of the sky, had encouraged Paul to remember with some pride that he was a twenty-first century European. Shah Shan had learned English far faster and much more fluently than Mylai Tui. By skilfully stimulating his teacher, he had precipitated Paul into journeying back through space and time to his own world. Shah Shan had a flair for grasping intuitively. With remarkably few words, Paul could create a scene for him—whether in a London street or on a rocket launching pad or on an East Anglian farm—that was both vivid and immediate. Under a joint spell of perception, they could together travel far and recreate much, while Mylai Tui was left hopelessly behind—lost in a welter of complex and meaningless words.

It was then Paul had discovered that, despite her discipline and training as a noia in the Temple of Gaiety, she was inclined to be jealous and possessive. She wanted the stranger for herself. At first her possessiveness amused him. Then it began to annoy him.

Oddly enough, Mylai Tui had displayed another aspect of her strange temper for the first time a few days before Enka Ne—or Shah Shan—was due to die. It had been caused by the incident Paul had witnessed on the morning he had walked along the Canal of Life to sit down and stare idly at the toilers in the kappa fields.

Although he had promised the woman who had given birth to her baby on the other side of the mound where he was sitting that he would 'unsee what he had seen,' he had taken the promise literally only insofar as not mentioning the place or the time to anyone. He would not betray her, but neither would he attempt in the literal sense to unsee what he had seen. It was, perhaps, his most important discovery in Baya Nor.

Mylai Tui had three fingers and a thumb on each hand. Everyone else he had met had three fingers and a thumb on each hand. And, because of the command of Enka Ne at their first meeting, he himself now conformed, having had each of his little fingers struck off.

Consequently, he had assumed that three fingers was normal—biologically normal. But what if that were not entirely so? The woman on the other side of the mound had given birth to a baby with three fingers on one hand and four fingers on the other. How many more women in Baya Nor bore children with four fingers and a thumb on one of their hands? And, carrying the thought further, how many women bore children with four fingers and a thumb on each of their hands?

That day, after returning home, he had asked Mylai Tui to let him see her hands. It was then he realised that he had never looked at them closely—really closely—before. He inspected them, cursing his rudimentary knowledge of anatomy and bemoaning the fact that he did not have a magnifying glass.

Then he discovered that the bone bump on the

side of her left hand was perhaps a little longer and more uneven than the bump on the side of her right hand. He took her left hand again, staring at it intently. Surely, there was the faintest mark of a scar?

"Mylai Tui, did you ever have four fingers on this hand?" he had asked abruptly.

She had snatched the hand away from him as if he offered her a deadly insult. And she had stood there, shaking and trembling and staring at him with eyes wide with horror.

At first, he thought she had misunderstood him. "I ask only if you ever had four fingers on this hand," he had repeated.

"Defiler!" she screamed. "Outlander! Beast! Savage!"

Then she had fled from the house.

He was completely baffled. Time passed, night came, and he thought that perhaps she had gone for good. She did not return until shortly before dawn of the following day. Then she came back and woke him up peremptorily. She was carrying a long thin korshl—the Whip of Correction that was used on petty criminals.

"Oruri has condescended to give guidance," she said tonelessly. "I have offended my lord. The offence cannot remain. Grace me with one blow of the korshl for each of the fingers on my hands."

He was dumbfounded. "Mylai Tui, I cannot do this thing."

"That is my punishment," she said, "according to the wisdom of Oruri. Six blows from my lord— or I must leave this house where I have been shamed for ever."

He saw that she meant it. He did not wish to lose her. Still not understanding, he took the korshl.

"Lay heavy, lord," said Mylai Tui, presenting her back. "Oruri frowns upon a light penance."

He struck, but apparently he did not strike hard enough. For his kindness which, said Mylai Tui, she did not deserve, Oruri would graciously award her two extra blows.

Early in the morning and still heavy with sleep, Paul Marlowe found himself participating in a waking nightmare. Mylai Tui was clearly not to be satisfied until the blood ran down her back. Eventually, in desperation he did in fact draw blood. The sight of it dripping down to make small thin rivulets on her legs, seemed to give Mylai Tui considerable satisfaction.

When the prescribed punishment was over, she fainted. Since that time he had not dared to refer to her fingers again.

Now, as he sat on the verandah step, sipping his kappa spirit, he became suddenly filled with a great and impersonal sadness—not only for himself and Shah Shan and Mylai Tui, but for all living things on all possible worlds scattered throughout the black starlit vault of space. He was sad because of the very predicament of living. Because every living creature—like the guyanis, the brilliantly coloured butterfly that he had seen killed by a leathery bird when he travelled with Enka Ne along the Canal of Life—was doomed to journey from darkness to darkness, with only a brief burst of sunlight and pain between the two long aspects of eternity. The guyanis had died, then the bird who had killed it was struck down by a warrior, then the warrior himself died at the command of Enka Ne. Now Enka Ne was dead and another Enka Ne was alive. And doubtless many more guyanis butterflies had been torn to pieces by toothed beaks. And doubtless many more warriors had gone to the bosom of Oruri.

Multiply these things by a billion billion, square the number and square it again. The resulting figure would still not be big enough to tally all the tragedies, great and small, taking place throughout the universe during one billion billionth part of a second.

Yes, thought Paul, living was indeed a sad situation—only slightly less sad than dying.

The sun had set and the nine moons of Altair Five were swarming silently across the sky. They were not bright enough to cast nine distinct shadows. They merely coated the sadness of the world with a threadbare film of silver.

Suddenly, Paul dropped the calabash and stiffened. Coming along the dusty track leading to his house there was a youth clad in a tattered samu and carrying a begging bowl. There was something about the walk, something about the gaunt moon-silver features . . . Paul Marlowe realized that he was trembling.

"Oruri greets you," said the boy.

"The greeting is a blessing," responded Paul mechanically.

"Blessed also are they who have seen many wonders." The boy smiled. "I am ZuShan, the brother of Shah Shan. I am also the gift of Enka Ne."

## NINETEEN

IT WAS THE middle of the night. Mylai Tui was asleep. Paul was awake. Outside the house, Zu Shan was lying half awake and half asleep with three other boys on a rough pile of bedding in the skeleton of the school that he was helping to build for Poul Mer Lo, the teacher.

Almost five Bayani months had passed since Enka Ne the 610th had assumed his spiritual and temporal role. During that time he had consistently ignored Poul Mer Lo. The attitude of Enka Ne passed down through his council, his administration and his religious orders. It was as if those who controlled the destiny of Baya Nor had decided to unsee what they had seen.

All of which, thought Paul, was very strange,

For though he had intentionally kept out of the way of the new god-king, he had continued with his innovations. The school was one of them.

It had started really with Zu Shan, who was the first official pupil. Then, as Paul was wandering through the city one morning, he came across a beggar—a small boy of five or six who, even by Bayani standards, seemed exceedingly dull-witted. He did not even know his own name. Looking at him, seeing his ribs sticking out and the tight flesh clinging pathetically to the bones of his misshapen legs. Paul was more than ordinarily moved. He was quite accustomed to the sight of beggars in Baya Nor, for the economy was not prosperous and the organization of labour was atrocious.

But this small child—though there were others like him—appeared to possess a mute eloquence. He did not talk much with his lips. All real communication seemed at first to be made with his eyes. They alone seemed to tell his entire story—a common one. He came of a family that was too large, he was not old enough or strong enough to do useful work, and in desperation his parents had trained him to beg and consigned him to the care of Oruri.

Then the eyes had said 'Pick me up, take me home. Pick me up, take me home.' Impulsively, Paul had scooped up the bony bundle and had taken it back to Mylai Tui. The boy would never be able to walk properly, for the parents, with practical consideration for the child's career as a beggar, had broken the bones in both legs in several places, and they had knit together in a crazy and grotesque fashion.

Paul called the boy Nemo. He never did need to talk a great deal. It was not until later that Paul discovered he was a natural telepath.

After ZuShan and Nemo there came Bai Lut, a one-armed youth whose right arm had been struck off for persistent stealing. And after Bai Lut there was Tsong Tsong, who had been fished out of the Mirror of Oruri, more dead than alive and who could not or would not remember anything of his past—though, at the age of perhaps eleven, he could not have had much past to remember.

And that was entire complement of the Paul Marlow Extra-Terrestrial Academy for Young Gentlemen.

As he paced up and down the room, while the small night lamp sent up thin desultory spirals of smoke, Paul thought of his school and of his achievements—or lack of them. He thought of the many hours he had spent simply trying to teach that the earth was round and not flat. He thought of the seemingly endless number of dried kappa leaves he had covered with charcoal scrawl, trying to demonstrate that it was possible to record words in the form of writing. He had modified some of the conventional sounds of the letters in the Roman alphabet to accommodate the Bayani tongue and he had stuck to a more or less phonetic form of writing.

But, with the exception of little Nemo, who was just about capable of writing his own name and those of his companions, no one seemed to grasp that it was possible to assign a logical sequence of meanings to a few marks on some dried kappa leaves. Or that even if it were, the operation could have any conceivable use other than the gratification of Poul Mer Lo.

On more practical and amusing levels, however, there had been some successes. Zu Shan had developed a flair for building small gliders, Bai Lut was good at making kites, and Tsong Tsong had—with some help—fashioned a successful model windmill which he used, oddly enough, to power a fan.

The boys seemed fascinated by the idea of harnessing the wind. It was something they could understand. Perhaps in the end, thought Paul, he would achieve a transient immortality by introducing the wheel and the use of wind power to the inhabitants of Baya Nor.

But what else could he do? What else was he equipped to do?

He did not know. Nor did he know whether the new god-king was really ignoring him or merely waiting for the stranger, who had enjoyed the favour of his predecessor, to commit some offence that would justify his permanent removal.

The uncertainty by itself did not worry him too much. What did worry him was his own feeling of inadequacy, his growing mood of futility and, above all, his isolation. He had begun to think more and more of Earth. He had begun to live more and more in the past. He dreamed of Earth, he day-dreamed of Earth, he longed to be back on Earth.

If he couldn't develop some kind of mental discipline to shut Earth away in a tiny compartment of his mind, he would presently go quite crazy. And that would be the saddest joke of all—one demented psychiatrist, the sole survivor of the expedition to Altair Five.

Mylai Tui groaned in her sleep. He stopped pacing up and down and decided that he would try to get some sleep himself. He glanced at her in the dim light and noted vaguely that she was getting rather fat. Then he lay down by her side and closed his eyes.

He still could not sleep. Visions of Earth kept drifting into his mind. He tried to concentrate on the school and calculate how long it would take to build with the help of four boys, two of whom were crippled.

Long enough, perhaps, to bring Enka Ne the 610th to the stone of sacrifice. Or Poul Mer Lo to a state of melancholic withdrawal from which there would be no return.

He let his arm rest lightly on Mylai Tui, feeling the soft warm flesh of her breast rise and fall rhythmically. It gave him no comfort. He was still staring blankly at the mud cemented thatch of the ceiling when dawn came.

## TWENTY

Two workmen had just delivered a load of rough-hewn wood for strengthening the frame-work of the small school. Poul Mer Lo noted with satisfaction that the wood had been brought on a four-wheeled cart complete with a two-man harness. He also noted with even greater satisfaction that the small Bayanis took their cart very much for granted. They might have been accustomed to using such vehicles for years instead of only for a matter of months. Poul Mer Lo—and this was one of the days when he did not think it was such a bad thing to be Poul Mer Lo, the teacher—wondered how long it would be before some Bayani genius decided that the front pair of wheels, their axle linked to a guiding shaft, would be more efficiently employed if they could swing on a vertical pivot.

But perhaps a vertical pivot and guiding mechanism for the front axle-tree was as yet too revolutionary a concept—as revolutionary as differential gears might have been to an eighteenth-century European coach-builder. Perhaps it would require a few more generations before the Bayani themselves added refinements to the new method of transport that had been introduced by the stranger. Certainly, Poul Mer Lo decided, he would not present them with the device himself. It would be a mistake not to let the Bayani do some of their own discovering.

It was a warm, sunny morning. When they had unloaded their wood, the workmen rested a while, wiped the sweat from their foreheads and regarded with obvious amusement the crazy structure that was being built by two boys and two cripples. Poul Mer Lo gave them the copper ring he had promised, and there was much exchange of courtesies.

Then one of them said somewhat diffidently: "Lord, what is this thing that you cause these lost ones to raise? Is it, perhaps, to be a temple for the gods of your own country?"

"It is not to be a temple," explained Poul Mer Lo, "But a school." There was no word for school in the Bayani language so he simply introduced the English word.

"A sku-ell?"

"That is right," answered Poul Mer Lo gravely. "A school."

"Then for what purpose, lord, is this sku-ell to be raised?"

"It is to be a place where children come to learn new skills."

The Bayani scatched his head and thought deeply. "Lord, does not the son of a hunter learn to hunt and the son of a carver learn to carve?"

"That is so."

"Then, lord, you do not need this sku-ell," said the Bayani triumphantly, "for the young learn by watching the old, such is the nature of life."

"That is true," said Poul Mer Lo. "But consider. These are children now without fathers. Also the skills that they shall learn shall be skills such as their fathers have not known."

The Bayani was puzzled. "It is known that lost ones are the beloved of Oruri, from whom they will receive that which they are destined to receive . . . Also, lord, may not new skills be dangerous?"

"New skills may indeed be dangerous," agreed Poul Mer Lo, "but so also may old skills be dangerous. The school is where—with the blessing of Oruri—these lost ones may perhaps gather some small wisdom."

The Bayani was baffled, but he said politely: "Wisdom is good to have, lord—but surely Enka Ne is the source of wisdom?"

"Without doubt, Enka Ne is the greatest source of wisdom in Baya Nor," said Poul Mer Lo carefully, "but it is good, is it not, that lesser beings should endeavor to achieve wisdom?"

The Bayani urinated on the spot. "Lord, these matters are too great for poor men to consider . . . Oruri be with you." He signalled to his companion, and they picked up the harness of the cart.

"Oruri be with you always," responded Poul Mer Lo, "at the end as at the beginning."

He watched them as they trundled the cart back along the Road of Travail towards the Third Avenue of the Gods.

For a while he supervised the stacking of the timber. Then, because the day was hot, he sat down to rest in the shadow of the small patch of roofing already on top of the school house.

Presently Nemo scuttled towards him, sideways, legs all twisted and arms used as forelegs, like some pathetic hybrid of crab and baboon. His small wizened face was creased in an expression of perplexity.

"Lord, I may speak with you?" asked the child formally.

"Yes, Nemo, you may speak with me."

The boy circled in the dust, vainly endeavouring to make himself comfortable.

"Lord, in the night that has passed my head was filled with strange creatures and strange voices. I am troubled. It is said that those who listen to the people of the night go mad."

Poul Mer Lo gazed at him curiously. "Tell me first of the creatures."

"I do no know whether they were animals or men, lord," said Nemo. "They were encased in a strange substance that caught the sunlight and became a thing of fire, as sometimes does the surface of water when a man sits by the Mirror of Oruri. They were tall, these beings, and they walked upon two legs. The skin of their head was smooth and hard like ring money. In their heads they carried weapons or tools. Truly they were terrible to behold. Also their god was with them."

"Their god?" echoed Poul Mer Lo blankly.

"Yes, lord, for such a being could only be a god."

"Describe this god, then."

"It was many times the height of many men, lord. It came down from the sky, walking upon a column of fire that scorched the white earth, transforming it into great clouds of steam and a torrent of water. Then, when the steam had subsided and the water was no more, the god opened his belly and brought forth many tall children—those whose skin was as fire in the sunlight."

Poul Mer Lo was trembling. He was also sweating profusely. And, sweating and trembling, he could visualize the scene almost as clearly as Nemo.

"Tell me more," he said hoarsely. "Tell me more of this vision that came to you in the night."

"Lord there is no more to tell. I saw and was afraid."

"What of the voices, then?"

Nemo frowned with concentration. "The voices did not seem to come from the creatures, lord. They came from the god."

"Try to remember, Nemo, what they said. It is important."

The boy smiled. "They, at least, did not frighten me, lord; for they spoke chiefly in riddles."

Poul Mer Lo wiped the sweat from his forehead and forced himself to be calm. If he could not stay calm he would never get the rest of the story from Nemo. And it was important that he should learn all that the boy knew. It was more important than anything else in his life.

"Tell me these riddles, Nemo, for it may be that I shall understand."

Nemo looked at him curiously. "Lord, are you ill or tired? I should not weary you with my unimportant thoughts if you are not well."

Poul Mer Lo made a great effort to control himself. "It is nothing, Nemo. I am in good health. Your story interests me . . . What were these riddles?"

Nemo laughed. "All men are brothers," he said. "That, surely, is a fine riddle, lord, is it not?"

"Yes, Nemo, it is a very good riddle. What else?"

"There are lands beyond the sky where the seed of man has taken root . . . That, too, is very funny."

"It is indeed funny . . . Is that all?"

"No, lord. There is one more riddle—the most amusing. It is that some day the god with the tail of fire will unite all the children of all the lands beyond the sky into a family which will be numberless, as are the drops of water in the Mirror of Oruri."

"Nemo," said Poul Mer Lo quietly, "what you have dreamed is a most wonderful dream. I cannot understand how these things could be made known to you. But I believe that there is much truth in what you have seen and heard. I hope that you will have such dreams again. If that happens—if you should again receive the grace of Oruri—I hope also that you will tell me all that you can remember."

Nemo seemed relieved. "These afflictions will not bring madness, then?"

Poul Mer Lo laughed—and tried vainly to suppress the note of hysteria in his voice. "No, they will not bring madness, Nemo. Nor are they afflictions. They are the gift of Oruri."

At that point Mylai Tui came from the house with a calabash and a jug of watered kappa spirit. Seeing her, Nemo scuttled away. He and Mylai Tui hated each other. Their hatred was the product of jealousy.

"Paul," said Mylai Tui gaily in English. "I wish you to drink. I wish you to drink as I drink, so that the joy will be shared."

She poured some of the watered kappa spirit into the calabash then raised it to her own lips and handed it to him. She seemed happier than she had been for many, many days.

"What is this joy of which you speak?" he said haltingly in Bayani. His head was reeling.

"Oruri has looked upon us," explained Mylai Tui.

"I am no wiser."

Mylai Tui laughed. "My lord, you are great with wisdom but not with perception." She pirouetted. "Whereas I," she continued, "am now indisputably great with child."

## TWENTY-ONE

IT WAS IN the seventh month of the reign of Enka
Ne the 610th that the forest tribe known to the
people of Baya Nor as the Lokhali attacked the
temple of Baya Lys. Although Baya Lys was three
days' journey from Baya Nor overland, it was only
one full day's journey away on the Canal of Life.
Apart from the ignominy of having a temple dese-
crated and its priestly occupants put to death in
various dreadful ways, the Bayani felt that this
warlike tribe was getting too near to the sacred city
for comfort.

Accordingly, Enka Ne declared a holy war. The
standing army of Baya Nor was swollen by volunteers; and when the oracle decreed that the time
and circumstances were propitious for victory,

over two thousand men moved off into the forest along the overland route.

Poul Mer Lo had asked to be allowed to go with them, not because he had any desire to participate in the kind of bloody vengeance that the Bayani were eagerly anticipating, but because he remembered the last evening of the religious progress on which he had been permitted to accompany Enka Ne the 609th.

While he was spending a restless night in one of the guest cells of Baya Lys, Shah Shan had come to him, bringing a bundle that had contained one plastic visor, two atomic grenades and a wrecked transceiver. These, said Shah Shan, had been found by the priests of Baya Lys near a blackened hole in the forest—in territory that was near to the land occupied by the Lokhali.

When Poul Mer Lo had suggested that Enka Ne might treat with the Lokhali to obtain news of any survivors from the *Gloria Mundi*, Shah Shan had rejected the idea instantly. The Lokhali, he had explained, lived for war. Not only was it impossible to have peaceful relations with them, but it was also beneath the dignity of the superior and civilized people of Baya Nor.

There the matter had ended. Since that time, Poul Mer Lo had not pressed his suggestion, knowing that in matters of this nature even Enka Ne, alias Shah Shan, had a closed mind.

But now the Lokhali had broken the uneasy state of peace—or, more accurately, non-war— that had existed between them and the Bayani. It was a golden opportunity for going along with the avenging army and trying to discover if any of the

Lokhali had encountered any survivors of the *Gloria Mundi*. Twelve people had travelled in the star ship. Three were accounted for. But of the remaining nine there had been no news whatsoever. The forest might have swallowed them. Or the occupants of the forest. There was no trace of them save the relics that Shah Shan had brought to the guest cell at Baya Lys.

Poul Mer Lo's application was rejected. It was rejected in person by Enka Ne in the Temple of the Weeping Sun.

It was the first and last time Poul Mer Lo had audience with Enka Ne the 610th. Unlike his predecessor, he was an old, old man. The ceremonial plumage lay ill upon him. His bird cry was thin and reedy. He strutted sadly, like one who was too heavily burdened with care and responsibility—which, probably, was the case.

"I am told you are a teacher, Poul Mer Lo," he had said.

"Yes, lord, that is so."

"It is the province of a teacher to teach, is it not?"

"Yes, lord."

"Then teach, Poul Mer Lo, and leave more weighty matters to those who know how best to deal with them. The hunter should remain with his darts, the warrior with his trident, and the teacher with his—what is the word you have given us?—sku-ell."

Then Enka Ne uttered his desolate bird cry, indicating that the audience was at an end. As Poul Mer Lo withdrew, he heard the god-king vainly trying to stifle a paroxysm of coughing.

The expedition against the Lokhali was brief and successful. After eleven days, the victorious army—minus about four hundred and fifty casualties—returned to Baya Nor with nearly one hundred prisoners.

Enka Ne addressed the prisoners at considerable length in the sacred city, regardless of the fact that they could not understand a word of what he was saying. Then he decreed that every eighth man should be set free, without food or weapons, to make his way back—if he could—to the land of the Lokhali, there to report on the clemency and omnipotence of Enka Ne. The remainder were to be crucified on the Fourth Avenue of the Gods to demonstrate the vengeance of Oruri and the unprofitability of attacking Bayani Temples.

On the day of crucifixion, which had been declared a day of celebration and rejoicing, Poul Mer Lo, in common with several thousand Bayani, strolled along the Fourth Avenue of the Gods.

Apart from the fact that nearly ninety men were dying in a slow and altogether gruesome manner, the scene was vaguely reminiscent of a terrestrial fair or carnival. Cheap-jacks were offering various delicacies and novelties, jinricksha men—using two-wheeled carriages, by grace of the stranger, Poul Mer Lo—were doing a roaring trade in slow journeys between the rows of wooden crosses. And children were working off their surplus energies by pelting the dying Lokhali with stones, offal and small aromatic missiles compounded of excreta.

Poul Mer Lo, steeling himself against the suffering, passed the dying Lokhali, one by one, and tried to observe them with scientific detachment.

He failed. The stench and the pain and the cries were too much for him. He did nót even notice that they were all taller than the Bayani or that most of them possessed four fingers and a thumb.

However, as he passed one who was clearly *in extremis*, he heard a few words—half murmured, half moaned—that stopped him in his tracks and brought back visions of a world that he would never see again.

*"Grüss Gott,"* sobbed the Lokhali, *"Grüss Gott!* Thank you . . . Thank you . . .*'chantez de faire votre connaissance'* . . . Man . . . Woman . . . Good morning . . . Good night. Hello! Hello! Hello!"

"Where are they?" demanded Poul Mer Lo in Bayani.

There was no response.

"Where are they—the strangers?" he repeated in English.

Again there was no response.

*"Ou est les étrangers?"*

Suddenly the Lokhali's body jerked spasmodically. Then he gave a great cry and hung slackly on the wooden cross.

In a fury of frustration, Poul Mer Lo began to shake the corpse.

But there was no miracle of resurrection.

## TWENTY-TWO

PAUL MARLOWE was no longer quite so dissatisfied with his 'Extra-Terrestrial Academy'. In the last few months both Zu Shan and Nemo had made quite remarkable progress. Once Paul had managed to convince them that it was both a privilege and a pleasure for any thinking person to find out as much as possible about the world in which he exists, and that knowledge brought the power to accomplish much that could not be otherwise achieved, the boy and the crippled child became filled with insatiable curiosity.

It was as if something had exploded in their minds, sweeping away all the inhibitions, the close-thought attitudes, and the deadening traditions of centuries of Bayani culture. The sophisticated savages became primitive scientists. They no longer accepted what they were told. They challenged it, they tried to refute it, they asked awkward questions. By Earth standards, Zu Shan was about fifteen—three or four years younger than his dead brother—and Nemo could not be more than six. Yet hardship and suffering had brought them a premature maturity. So that when they did eventually grasp the importance of learning, they began to learn at a very high speed.

The same could not be said of either the one-armed Bai Lut or Tsong Tsong. They did not have the spark. Their minds would never get into top gear. Temperamentally, they were hewers of wood and drawers of water. They lacked imagination—and that strange ability to take an intuitive leap into the dark. They were content to play with toys, whereas Zu Shan and Nemo, though not above playing with toys, also wished to play with ideas.

Zu Shan, sensing perhaps that there was more to be got from his teacher than could properly be expressed in Bayani, began to learn English. Nemo, not to be outdone, also elected to learn what was for all practical purposes a 'dead tongue'.

But, besides providing the means for expressing new concepts, it gave them a sense of status to be able to talk to Paul in his own language. It gave them, too, a sense of intimacy, and drew the three of them close together.

Zu Shan was never quite as fluent as his brother in speaking the language of the stranger; but he soon learned enough to say all that he needed to say—if he took his time about it. Nemo, though younger, had an advantage. He had already discovered that on occasion he could establish sufficient *en rapport* to read minds.

The three of them were sitting on the verandah step one evening while Paul sipped his kappa spirit. It had been a hard but pleasant day, for they had completed the building of the school. It contained chairs and tables, a potter's wheel, a small furnace for baking pots, a few kappa leaf charts and some tools that the boys had designed themselves. It also contained four rough beds. It was the first boarding school in Baya Nor.

"You are looking far away, Paul," said Zu Shan. "What are you thinking about?"

Nemo smiled. "He is thinking about many things," he announced importantly. "He is thinking about the stars, and about the words of the dying Lokhali soldier, and about the star ship in which he came to Altair Five, and about a white-skinned woman. I have been riding his thoughts, but there are so many different ones that I keep falling off."

Nemo's favourite description for his telepathic exercise was 'riding thoughts'. To him it seemed a very accurate description; for he had discovered that people do not think tidily, and that their mental processes are frequently disjointed—which was why he could not receive for very long without 'falling off'.

Paul laughed as the tiny, crippled Bayani recited the revealing catalogue. "You will get yourself into trouble one of these days, Nemo," he observed. "You will ride a thought which tells you that I am about to drop you into the Canal of Life."

"Then I shall try to avoid the disaster," retorted Nemo complacently.

"Have you had any new dreams recently about the god who brought forth strange children from his belly?"

"No, only the old dream. I have it quite frequently now. I'm getting used to it."

Paul sighed. "I wish you could arrange to dream in greater detail. I wish, too, that I knew where you got the dream from. It could, I suppose, be something you have picked up out of my dreams."

Nemo rolled his oddly ancient eyes. "Lord," he said in Bayani, "I would not dare to trespass in your sleeping journeys."

Suddenly Zu Shan sat upright. "I have just remembered something that may explain Nemo's dream," he said. "Have you ever heard the legend of the coming, Paul?"

"No. Tell me about it."

"It is a story that mothers tell their children," went on Zu Shan. "It must be very, very old . . . You know, of course, that Oruri can take many shapes?"

"Yes."

"The story goes that long ago there were no people at all in the land of Baya Nor—I mean, on Altair Five—but that Oruri looked down on this world and saw that it was good. Therefore he came and stood on a white mountain and looked over the land. And out of his great happiness, many people were born, and they walked down from the mountain to play as children in the new world that Oruri had found. According to the legend, Oruri stands waiting on the white mountain. He is waiting until the people are tired of their play. Then they will go back to him and he will return with them to the world from which he came.''

''It is a good legend,'' commented Paul, taking a draught of his kappa spirit. ''The plot thickens, does it not?''

''What do you mean, Paul?''

''Only that I cannot help seeing Oruri as a star ship . . . I think too much of star ships, these days . . . And yet . . . And yet Nemo dreams of creatures in strange metallic clothing. And his god descends on a column of fire as a star ship would. And the god opens his belly . . .''

''Paul.''

''Yes, Zu Shan?''

''If the hunters are to be believed there is such a mountain—many days' travel to the north. They call it the Temple of the White Darkness. They say it is protected by strange voices, and that a man may approach it but the voices will either turn him back or drive him mad. They say that if he is courageous enough to approach the mountain, he will only stiffen and die.''

Paul Marlowe took another drink of the kappa spirit. ''I am not surprised, Zu Shan. I am not at all surprised . . . You have never seen snow, have you?''

''No, you have told us about it. But I don't think there is anyone in Baya Nor who has ever seen it.''

Paul felt suddenly elated and happy. Maybe it was the kappa spirit. Or maybe . . .

''Do you know,'' he said, after a brief silence. ''I think you two are going to make history. I think you are going to see snow.'' He hiccupped.

"Damn it, I wonder how much ring money I shall need to buy the services of half a dozen really good hunters?"

"Paul," said Zu Shan, "I do not think there is enough ring money in Baya Nor to persuade six hunters to go through the Lokhali country towards the Temple of the White Darkness."

"I have something better than ring money," said Paul. "It is about time I showed you my sweeper rifle. Your brother, who permitted me to keep it, is the only Bayani who has ever seen what it can do."

## TWENTY-THREE

UNINTENTIONALLY, THE one-armed Bai Lut, a
youth without any great degree of intelligence or
initiative, changed the course of history not only
on Altair Five but on many worlds about which he
would never know. He changed the course of history by building a kite. It was a beautiful kite
constructed of slivers of springy yana wood and
with the wind-catching surfaces painstakingly
woven from musa reed which, when separated
into its fibres, was used to weave musa loul, the
only kind of cloth known to the Bayani.

The kite had taken Bai Lut many days to make.
It was in the shape of a giant guyanis butterfly. Bai
Lut had dreamed of building such a kite for a long
time. Having only one arm, he had to work hard
with his toes as well as his fingers. When it was

finished, he regarded his achievement with awe. It was truly beautiful. He would have been quite content to die after such an achievement—or, at least, after he had seen it fly successfully—for it did not seem possible to do anything greater in life.

He prayed for a smooth, steady wind. His prayer was answered. And, with about two hundred metres of 'string' made from twisted hair—which had taken longer to manufacture than the kite itself—he flew the musa-winged guyanis and watched it soar joyously over the Canal of Life and lean high, almost yearningly, over the Mirror of Oruri towards the sacred city.

It may be that Bai Lut had prayed too ardently to Oruri for a wind. Because, when all of Bai Lut's string was extended and the kite was as high as it could go, a great gust came—so suddenly that the string snapped.

It was a tribute to Bai Lut's craftsmanship and intuitive grasp of aerodynamics that the guyanis kite did not immediately spiral down into the Mirror of Oruri. Instead it began to execute graceful curves, losing little altitude, but gliding almost purposefully towards the sacred city. Presently it was no more than a slowly descending speck in the sky. Presently it was out of sight.

And then the wind dropped, and the kite dropped. But Bai Lut did not know where to look for it. He was miserable with the conviction that he would never see it again. And in that he was right. For it had come to rest in the Temple of the Weeping Sun; and, though he fortunately did not know it, the guyanis kite had fallen on the stone phallus of sacrifice.

The following day, Poul Mer Lo was giving a lesson in school to his four pupils on basic mechanics and specifically on the use of the lever. He had demonstrated how a lever could be employed to do work that a man alone could not accomplish and was about to embark on the theory of the calculation of forces when he was interrupted by Nemo.

"Lord," said the tiny cripple formally in Bayani, "the warriors of Enka Ne are approaching along the Road of Travail."

Poul Mer Lo looked at the small boy in surprise. He was surprised not only by the interruption but by the formal method of address.

"The warriors of Enka Ne pass many times along the Road of Travail, Nemo. What has this to do with that which now concerns us?"

"Lord," said Nemo in some agitation. "I have been riding the thoughts of the captain. The warriors are coming here. They are in a hurry. I think they will arrive very soon."

Poul Mer Lo tried not to betray his anxiety. "In which case, we will pass the time considering how this instrument that I have shown you may be used to ease the burden of man."

"Paul," said Nemo desperately, breaking into English, "there is something very strange in the mind of the captain. He is thinking of a guyanis butterfly and the Temple of the Weeping Sun . . . It—it is very close now . . . I—I keep falling off."

"Do not be afraid, Nemo," said Paul gently. "No one here has done anything of which he need be afraid."

But in that he was wrong.

A Bayani warrior, armed with ceremonial trident, appeared in the doorway. His eyes flickered over the children, then came to rest on Paul.

"Oruri greets you," said the warrior truculently.

"The greeting is a blessing," responded Paul.

"Lord, I am the voice and hand of Enka Ne. Which of your lost ones fashioned the guyanis that was not a guyanis?"

"I do not know what —" began Paul.

But Bai Lut sprang importantly to his feet. "I am the maker of the guyanis," he announced. "Truly it was a thing of much power. Can it be that Enka Ne has observed—"

"Enka Ne observes all that is worthy of observation," cut in the warrior. "The flight of the guyanis was not well omened . . . Die now—and live for ever." Expertly he flung his short trident. The prongs struck deep in Bai Lut's throat. He fell over backwards, gurgled briefly and lay still.

For a moment or two Paul was stunned. He looked helplessly at the three horrified children then at the Bayani. Meanwhile, more warriors had filed into the school.

"Lord," said the captain, "it is the will of Enka Ne that you and these lost ones must withdraw from this place."

"But surely there cannot be any—"

"Lord," said the Bayani sternly, "Enka Ne has spoken. Let there be no more dying than the god-king commands."

Paul looked helplessly at Zu Shan and Nemo and Tsong Tsong, and then at the sad and bloody heap that was once Bai Lut, and finally at the dozen or so warriors waiting patiently behind their captain.

"Come," he managed to say at length in a voice that was extraordinarily calm, "what Enka Ne commands, it is fitting that we should obey."

He led the boys out between ranks of Bayani warriors. About twenty paces away from the school, they stood watching and waiting and listening as the warriors of Enka Ne smashed tables, chairs and all the carefully constructed equipment.

Presently they heard the captain say: "Make fire."

And presently the Bayani soldiers trooped out of the school as tell-tale spirals of smoke began to drift from under its eaves.

The dry wood burned quickly and fiercely and noisily. The heat forced everyone back; but the Bayani warriors remained until Bai Lut's funeral pyre was no more than a heap of glowing ashes.

The captain turned to Poul Mer Lo. "Such is the will of Enka Ne," he said.

If Bai Lut had not made the guyanis kite, if the wind had not broken his hair string, if the boy had not been so casually killed and the school burned down, Paul Marlowe would probably not have summoned sufficient determination to make the journey to the Temple of the White Darkness.

And it was the journey, and the timing of the journey, that changed the course of history.

## TWENTY-FOUR

WITH THE KNOWLEDGE that she was pregnant, Mylai Tui had become happy; and her happiness had grown in direct proportion to the increase in the size of her belly. Not even the death of Bai Lut and the burning of the school could diminish it greatly; these were things about which she cared only because they were things about which Paul Marlowe cared.

She was happy not only with the simple feminine satisfaction of biological fulfilment. She was happy with the uniqueness of bearing a son—obviously it was to be a son, for a girl would not kick so lustily—for one who had ridden on the wings of a silver bird from a land beyond the sky. Fortunate was she whom Oruri had chosen to be the vessel of the seed of him who had the gift of greatness.

She looked at Paul with pride. He was taller than any in Baya Nor; and though his skin, despite much exposure to the sun, was still sadly pale and far from the desired black of the Bayani of ancient lineage, he was very much a man—as his thanu and vigorous muscles testified. Such a one must surely beget a son in his own image. And then Mylai Tui would be a woman whom all other women could only envy.

Her happiness and her anticipatory daydreams, however, were short-lived. They came to an end on the evening that Paul told her of his determination to make the journey to the Temple of the White Darkness.

"Paul," she pleaded in bad English, "you cannot do this thing. Are you so sad that only death will end the sadness?"

"It has nothing to do with sadness," he explained patiently. "There are mysteries which I must try to unravel. And it seems that the mountain may at least provide another clue . . . I shall go as soon as I can find hunters to go with me."

"You will not find any," she said, lapsing into Bayani. "There are none so foolish in Baya Nor as to wish to venture into the bosom of Oruri before they are called."

Laughing, he, too, spoke in Bayani: "Courage, pride and greed—these are the things that will give me the hunters I want. The journey will appeal to their courage. Their pride will be challenged because I, a stranger, am not afraid to make this journey. And the twenty copper rings that I shall offer to each man will be sufficient to overcome any falterings of courage . . . Besides, there is the

weapon I brought with me and which I was permitted to keep by Enka Ne. It lies, now, wrapped
in musa loul and buried in a box of hard wood.
When I show the hunters its power, they will have
no doubts.''

''You will have to pass the Lokhali, lord. The
people of Baya Nor do not fear the Lokhali—but
neither do the Bayani pass through their country,
unless it be as an army.''

''Yes, we shall have to pass the Lokhali. But,
Mylai Tui, with the weapon I brought from the
other side of the sky, we shall be as an army.''

''My lord, the weapon did not prevent you from
entering the donjons of Baya Nor.''

''It did not.'' Again he laughed. ''But who may
question the purpose of Oruri?''

Mylai Tui was silent for a moment or two. Then
she said: ''None have ventured to the mountain
and returned.''

There are those who have seen the mountains
and returned.

She gave him a look of sad resignation. ''Lord, I
know there is much about you that I cannot understand and much that I will never understand. I am
proud to have lain with you, and I am proud to
have received at last the gift of your loins. If it
pleases my lord to seek Oruri before Oruri does the
seeking, then I will endeavour to accept this thing
. . . But stay, my lord, stay long enough to look
upon the face of your son.''

He took her hands. ''Mylai Tui, I know it is hard
for you to understand. But my head is sorely troubled by many questions. This thing will not wait. I
must go as soon as I may, and I must see what can

be seen. But I will return. I will return because I greatly desire to lie with you, as I will lie with you this night. And I will return because I desire greatly to gaze upon the harvest of the joining of our flesh . . . Now let there be an end. The decision is made. Zu Shan seeks the hunters, and I doubt not that they will be found."

Suddenly, she brightened. "It is possible, is it not, that Enka Ne may learn of this madness and prevent it?"

Paul gave her a penetrating look. "I respect the power of Enka Ne. Let the god-king respect mine. Otherwise, many in Baya Nor may have cause to grieve."

Three days later, in the early evening, when the nine moons rode high and swiftly through a cloudless sky, Zu Shan brought four hunters to the house of Poul Mer Lo. The usual courtesies were exchanged and the men squatted in a semi-circle on the verandah while Mylai Tui supplied them with kappa spirit.

"Paul," said Zu Shan in English, so that the Bayani would not understand, "These are the men we should take. There were others attracted by the payment you offered. But these are the best. Two of them I already knew, and the others are known to them. They are among the best hunters in Baya Nor. But more than that, they have much faith in Poul Mer Lo, the teacher. And one of them, Shon Hu, has even seen the mountain. He has hunted very far, and he says he knows the way."

"Are they afraid?"

Zu Shan gave a thin smile. "Yes, Paul, they are afraid—as I am."

"Good. Men who are afraid live longer. You have done very well, Zu Shan—better than I thought."

He turned to the Bayani, who were politely sipping their kappa spirit as though no one had spoken.

"Hunters," said Poul Mer Lo in Bayani, "I journey far. It may be that there will be danger on this journey, for I am told that the Temple of the White Darkness is not a place where men go who wish to count the great number of their grandchildren."

The hunters laughed, a little self-consciously.

"But I think," went on Poul Mer Lo, "that we shall be among those who return; for if men desire something greatly, they can often accomplish it. Also, we shall carry a terrible weapon which I have brought with me for this purpose from the land beyond the sky."

"Lord," said the man who had been identified as Shon Hu, "the journey is one thing but the Lokhali is another."

Poul Mer Lo rose, went into the house and returned with his sweeper rifle.

"Your darts and blow-pipes, your tridents and clubs are excellent weapons," he said. "But how many Lokhali can you stop with them if we are attacked?"

Shon Hu looked at his companions. "Lord, we are only men—good men, perhaps, but no more than men. Perhaps, if Oruri smiled, we would carry three times our own number of Lokhali with us into his bosom."

Poul Mer Lo pushed the breeder button of his

atomic rifle. About two hundred metres away there was a small group of trees looming in the twilight.

"Observe!" said Poul Mer Lo. He sighted, pressed the trigger and swept the tops of the trees with the rifle. After two or three passes, smoke began to rise. After five passes, the trees burst into flame—a noisy, crackling bonfire.

"Lord," said Shon Hu at length, "you have shown us a fearful thing."

"It is," agreed Poul Mer Lo, "a most fearful thing. Your job Shon Hu, will be to protect me. My job will be to use this weapon. If we are attacked by the Lokhali, many of them will need to explain to Oruri why they wished to obstruct the passing of Poul Mer Lo and his companions . . . " He gazed round the semi-circle. "Nevertheless, I know our journey is still a difficult and dangerous one. If any of you feels that he has spoken rashly, let him now stand and go forth. We who remain will pray for the good fortune of his children and his children's children."

No one moved.

Silently and sadly, Mylai Tui brought more kappa spirit.

# TWENTY-FIVE

AFTER MUCH HARD bargaining, Shon Hu had obtained a barge for the very reasonable sum of nine rings. Poul Mer Lo, impatient to get the expedition under way now that he had made his decision, would have paid the sixteen rings demanded by the barge builder without question. But, as Shon Hu explained, to have paid such a price without haggling would have excited much interest. The barge builder would have boasted of his achievement, enquiries might then have been made about Shon Hu, the actual purchaser, and the ring money might then have been traced back to Poul Mer Lo. That in itself might well have been sufficient to bring the transaction to the notice of one of the officers of the god-king; and, quite possibly, the whole expedition would have been frustrated before it had begun. For, after the burning of the school, it was obvious that Enka Ne was not so oblivious of the activities of the stranger as Poul Mer Lo had formerly supposed.

So he had to wait patiently for two full days while Shon Hu and a phenomenal quantity of kappa spirit brought the price down to nine rings.

The time was not wholly wasted, however, for there was much to be done. Supplies of fresh water had to be stored in skins, as had quantities of dried kappa and smoked strips of meat; for though the expedition included four hunters, Poul Mer Lo did not propose to waste much time hunting for food. Of his personal possessions, he proposed to take only the transceiver and the sweeper rifle. The atomic grenades that Shah Shan had presented to him at the temple of Baya Lys were not suitable weapons for close range fighting—if, indeed, any close range fighting should occur. To call them weapons was not completely accurate, either, for they were far more use to engineers than soldiers—except, perhaps, where a very long fuse could be used as during a retreat, or for very long range work.

Poul Mer Lo did not really know why he was taking the transceiver. It was in excellent order; and its miniature 'hot' battery would remain efficient for a long time to come. But he well knew that there was no other working transmitter on Altair Five. During the last few months, many times at dead of night he had put the transceiver on full power and swept carefully through the medium and short wave bands. All he could raise was the usual random crackle.

The sweeper rifle gave him some cause for anxiety. There was a visual indicator showing its charge level, and this was now registering well below the half-charge mark; indicating that the rifle was now not good for more than half a dozen full strength discharges. Somehow, it had leaked; and as he did not possess a geiger counter there was no means of telling if the micro-pile were still intact. For all he knew, thought Poul Mer Lo, both he and the rifle might now be dangerously radioactive—a menace to all and sundry. But there was nothing to be done about it. If such were the will of Oruri . . . He was amused at himself for letting the expression creep into his train of thought.

Shon Hu said that it would be possible to travel by barge for two and a half days—one day along the Canal of Life and one and a half days upstream on the great river, which was known, picturesquely enough, as the Watering of Oruri. After that there would be perhaps two days, on the uplands. Shon Hu was vague about this latter stretch of the journey. All that he seemed certain about was that once the forest was left behind, the Temple of the White Darkness would be clearly visible. How it was to be approached was a matter upon which Oruri would doubtless provide guidance when the time came.

The expedition was to depart from Baya Nor at the first sign of light so that much poling could be done before the sun rose high in the sky. Also, such an early departure would be unlikely to attract the attention of anyone but hunters; for few Bayani cared to move before the sun was well clear of the horizon.

The barge was ready, laden with food, water, the blow pipes, darts and tridents of the hunters, the sweeper rifle and the transceiver, and a pile of skins for the use as bedding and then as clothing when the warm forest was left behind. Besides the four hunters, Poul Mer Lo was taking Zu Shan and Nemo with him. Tsong Tsong was to be left behind as company for Mylai Tui, and Poul Mer Lo had given her enough money to buy a girl servant to help in the house if the baby should arrive before he returned from the Temple of the White Darkness.

Nemo was the real problem. With his grotesquely deformed legs he could not possibly walk. Yet Poul Mer Lo did not wish to leave him behind—not only because the oddly ancient child desperately wanted to go with him but because Nemo's telepathic powers might prove useful. It was Nemo, with his visions of a god bringing forth children from his belly, who had triggered the whole thing off. Just possibly there might be something on the slopes of the white mountain. Just possibly Nemo might sense where and what that something was. Yes, he would have to go. And so a sling was made for him so that he could ride on the back of each of the hunters in turn.

The night before departure, the hunters, Nemo and Zu Shan slept on skins on the flat bottom of the barge. Poul Mer Lo did not sleep. Neither did

Mylai Tui. They lay close to each other and remote from each other in the small house that, over the months, had begun to acquire for Poul Mer Lo the sweetly subtle smell of home.

Mylai Tui was certain it was the last time they would hold each other.

"Lord," she said in Bayani, "I am fat, now, and can no longer pretend to possess some beauty. It is not fitting that a woman should speak thus—but I greatly desire that you should lie with me and try to remember how it once was."

He kissed her and fondled her. "Mylai Tui," he said, also speaking in the high Bayani that he knew she preferred, "to be with child does not diminish beauty, but changes the shape of beauty. I will remember how it once was. But how it now is is dear to me also. And this, too, I will remember."

They made love, but though there was great tenderness there was little passion. It had seemed strangely, thought Poul Mer Lo when it was over, more like a solemn ritual, dignifying or celebrating some unique event that had not happened before and would not happen again. He was puzzled and, for the first time, he was afraid.

"Lord," said Mylai Tui simply, "the fire is kindled, flourishes and dies. We shall not come to each other again. I wish to humbly thank you, for you have given me much joy . . . I do not have the gift of leaping thoughts like Shah Shan, whom I think you loved, and like some others whom, perhaps, you love in a lesser way. But if my thoughts could not leap, lord, my flesh leaped joyously. I am sad now that it will leap no more."

He held her very close. "I shall return from the Temple of the White Darkness," he whispered. "This I swear."

"If it is the will of Oruri," said Mylai Tui, dully. "My lord has the gift of greatness and can accomplish much."

"I shall return," he repeated fiercely.

Mylai Tui sighed. "But we shall come together no more. This I know. It is written on the water. It is written in the wind . . . Lay your hand on my belly, lord."

He did so, and was rewarded with a kick.

"Is not your son vigorous and mighty of limb like him that presented the seed?"

"Truly, he will be a fine child."

"Then go now, for the first light is with us. And remember, lord. Such as I am, I gave what I could. I will remember with pride that I carry the child of one who has ridden upon a silver bird. But go now, for the waters sting in my eyes, and I would not have you remember me thus . . . Oruri be with you—at the end as at the beginning."

"Oruri be with you always," responded Poul Mer Lo. He touched her forehead with his lips. Then he got up and quickly went from the house.

In the pre-dawn light, the world seemed very quiet and very lonely. He walked briskly down to the Canal of Life without looking back, and trying not to think of anything at all. But there was a taste of salt upon his lips, and he was amazed that non-existent tears could hurt so much.

## TWENTY-SIX

IT WAS GOING TO BE a hot day. The Canal of Life
lay placid and steaming with a light mist that held
close to its surface, drifting and swirling lazily in
the still air. Voices carried. From many paces
away, Poul Mer Lo could hear the low murmurings
of the hunters and the boys as they made ready for
the journey.

Excitement was in the tight atmosphere. Poul
Mer Lo felt almost that he could reach out his
hands and touch it as he stepped aboard the rough
but sturdy barge that was to carry them on the
journey. He pushed regret and doubt out of his
mind. He locked his last memories of Mylai Tui—
knowing now that they were indeed his last
memories of her—into some deep compartment of

his brain where they would be safe until he needed to take them out and dwell upon them.

"Lord," said Shon Hu, "we have eaten and are ready. Speak only the word."

Poul Mer Lo glanced round the small craft and saw six faces gazing at him expectantly. "As this journey begins," he said formally, "though it be long or short, easy or most hard, let all here know that they are as brothers to help each other in difficulty and to rejoice or suffer with each other according to the will of Oruri . . . Let us go, then."

The hunters turned to the sides of the barge and urinated into the Canal of Life. Then they took up their poles and pushed away from the bank. Presently the barge was gliding smoothly over the still, mist-covered water; and as the sun rose above the edge of the forest, bringing with it new textures and forms, and intensifying colours, Poul Mer Lo began to feel for the first time since his arrival on Altair Five an odd lightness of heart. So far, he thought, he had been chiefly a spectator—despite his introduction of the wheel into the Bayani culture and despite his sporadic efforts to fulfil the prediction of the oracle that he would be a great teacher. But now, he felt, he was really doing something.

Whether the legend of the coming and Nemo's dreams amounted to anything did not really matter. Whether there were any spectacular discoveries to be made at the Temple of the White Darkness did not really matter. What did matter was that he had managed to break through the centuries old Bayani mood of insularity. For so long, they had cultivated the habit of not wanting to know. They had been content with their tiny static society in a small corner of the forests of Altair Five.

But now things were different; and whatever happened there could be no permanent return to the *status quo*. The hunters, he realized, were not coming with him for the ring money alone. Nor were they coming because of blind faith in Poul Mer Lo. They were coming basically because their curiosity had been aroused—because they, too, wished to find out what was in the next valley or over the next mountain.

They did not know it, but they were the first genuine Bayani explorers for centuries . . . All that I have done, thought Poul Mer Lo, and perhaps the most important thing that I have done, is to help make such a mental climate possible.

Which turned his mind automatically to Enka Ne. For hundreds of years the god-kings of Baya Nor had—consciously or otherwise—maintained their absolute authority and absolute power by inhibiting curiosity. This Shah Shan had realized. He had had the wisdom to encourage Poul Mer Lo, whom the councillors and the priests of the blind order regarded as an instrument of chaos because he asked questions that had not previously been asked, and did things that had not previously been done.

But the Enka Ne who came after Shah Shan was of a different temperament altogether. For one thing he was old. Perhaps in his youth, he, too, had possessed an enquiring mind. But if so, it had been crushed by his elders and by the ritualistic Bayani approach to life. Now that he was old, he stood clearly and decisively for orthodoxy.

As the barge left the kappa fields and the cleared land behind, passing under the great green umbra of the forest, Poul Mer Lo wondered idly if Enka Ne knew of his expedition. It was highly probable; for though Zu Shan had been very cautious in his recruitment of hunters, he had talked to several who had rejected the invitation. They, in turn, must have talked to others; and it was quite likely that an embroidered description of the expedition had now reached the ears of the god-king.

But now; thought Poul Mer Lo comfortably, it was too late to prevent the journey; and, in any case, if the god-king were as clever—despite his orthodoxy—as Poul Mer Lo suspected, he would not wish to prevent it. He would be somewhat relieved that the stranger had chosen to seek the bosom of Oruri far from Baya Nor.

Presently the barge passed the forest temple of Baya Sur without incident. There was no one at the landing place to witness its passing, since no one knew of its coming. And so the small craft sped on, deep into the forest to where the Canal of Life joined the Watering of Oruri.

The sun had passed its zenith before the hunters were ready to abandon their poles and take food and rest. They pulled in to the bank of the canal where there was a very small clearing and threw the anchor stone overboard.

Poul Mer Lo was glad of the opportunity to stretch his legs. He had offered to take turns with the poles, as Zu Shan had done; but the hunters had rejected his offer with great politeness. He was Poul Mer Lo, the stranger, unaccustomed to

the ways and rhythms of watermen. He was also
their employer and captain; and therefore it would
be unthinkable to let him do menial tasks except *in
extremis*.

When they had eaten, Poul Mer Lo, Zu Shan
and two of the hunters dozed. Nemo and the remaining two kept watch against wild animals for
there were many carnivorous beasts that hunted
by night and by day in the forest.

As he fell asleep, Poul Mer Lo was transformed
once more into Paul Marlowe—the Paul Marlowe
who lived and slept and endured suspended animation aboard the *Gloria Mundi*. He was on watch
with Ann, and he had just saved the occupants of
the star ship from death by explosive decompression after the hull of the ship had been penetrated
by small meteors. He tasted champagne once
more—*Moet et Chandon '11*, a very fine year.
Then there was some vague discussion on the nature of God . . .

The dream disintegrated as Nemo shook him.
For a terrible moment or two Paul did not know
where he was or recognize the wizened face of the
child.

"Lord," said Nemo in Bayani, "a barge follows
us. I think it is no more than ten flights of the dart
away. I ride the pole-men's thoughts. They are
seeking us. They have been offered many rings to
overtake us. Enka Ne has sent soldiers. Lord, I do
not think we can escape."

Paul Marlowe pulled himself together. He stood
up and looked at the barge. There did not seem to
be any way of camouflaging it or hiding it in time.
But he refused to accept defeat without doing

something. The only hope was to get out into the canal and pull like mad.

"Let us go quickly, then," he said to the hunters, who were gazing at him anxiously. "It is said that he who waits for trouble will be found by it most easily."

Within seconds the anchor stone was hauled up, the barge was in mid-stream and everyone— including Paul—was poling strenuously. Even Nemo, perched on the end of the barge, had a short pole with which, in the squatting position, he could provide a few extra pounds of thrust.

Unfortunately, the Canal of Life had few bends; and it was not long before the pursuers could see the pursued. Glancing over his shoulder, Paul saw that the following barge was a large one with sixteen pole-men and at least twice that number of warriors. It was gaining rapidly. In less than a minute it would be only the flight of a dart away— and if darts then began to fly, that would be the end of the matter.

"Stop poling!" he commanded, and picked up his sweeper rifle.

"Lord," said Shon Hu, "it seems that Oruri does not favour this enterprise. But speak the word and we will fight if we must."

"There will be no fighting," said Paul positively. "Take heart, Shon Hu. Oruri does but test us."

The pursuers, seeing that the men ahead of them had stopped poling, lifted their own poles and allowed the two craft to drift slowly towards each other.

Paul recognized the Bayani warrior standing in

the bows of the following barge. It was the captain who had been sent to execute Bai Lut and burn down the school.

"Oruri greets you!" called the captain.

"The greeting is a blessing," responded Paul.

"I am the voice and hand of Enka Ne. The god-king commands you to return to Baya Nor, there to give account of this journey."

"I am grieved that the god-king commands my presence, for this journey is most urgent and cannot wait."

The captain seemed amused. "Lord, I am commanded to enforce the command of Enka Ne, and that I will do most willingly."

Paul rested the sweeper rifle casually on his hip, his finger on the trigger. He had previously pushed the breeder button to full power discharge.

"Captain, listen to me for a moment. I wish you to return to Enka Ne and present my humble greetings, saying that I would that I could return to do his bidding, but that this matter cannot be delayed. If you return thus and in peace, the anger of Oruri will be withheld. I have spoken."

The captain laughed, his warriors laughed. Even the pole-men permitted themselves to grin.

"Brave words, my lord. But where is the strength behind the courage? You are few, we are many. As you will not come, then we must take you."

"So be it," said Paul. He pressed the trigger. The sweeper rifle whined, vibrating imperceptibly. The water immediately ahead of the following barge, which was still drifting slowly onwards, began to hiss and bubble to boiling point. It became turbulent, giving off great clouds of steam, then suddenly it was resolved into a great water spout. The barge, full of petrified soldiers and pole-men, drifted helplessly into the water spout. Immediately the wooden bows burst into flame, and the pressure of the water and steam capsized the heavily laden craft.

With cries of terror men and soldiers floundered in the Canal of Life. Paul had released the trigger as soon as the barge caught fire; but the patch of water continued to hiss and bubble for some moments. One poor wretch drifted near to it and was badly scalded.

"Thus," said Paul looking down at the captain struggling in the water, "the anger of Oruri comes to pass. Return now to Enka Ne and report this thing, giving him the words I have spoken." He turned to his own pole-men: "Let us continue, then. It seems that the warriors of the god-king will not hinder our passing."

Mechanically, and with looks of awe on their faces, the hunters took up their poles and got the small barge under way.

Shon Hu wiped the sweat from his face and glanced at the sweeper rifle. "Lord, with such power in his hands it seems that a man may become as a god."

Paul smiled. "No, Shon Hu. With such power in his hands, a man may only become a more powerful man."

## TWENTY-SEVEN

THE FOREST WAS ANCIENT, overwhelming and oppressive in its great green luxuriance. Amid all the noisy chatter of the wild things it contained, there were strange pockets of silence where it seemed to Paul Marlowe—never a connoisseur of forests, even on Earth—something intangible lay, lurking and brooding.

Perhaps it was the Life Force; for if a Life Force existed, surely the forest—a place teeming with crawly living things—must be its home. Of the large wild creatures, Paul did not see a great deal but he saw enough to make him feel that, in evolutionary terms, Altair Five must be at least a million years behind Earth.

Here and there, on the banks of the far reaches

of the Canal of Life, were colonies of large iguana-like animals—spiked, scaly, twice the length of a man and, so the hunters told him, virtually harmless. They were vegetarians. The only time they ever displayed ferocity was during a short mating season—and then only to others of their kind. On the other hand, there were small, delicate crab-like creatures—bright red and remarkably attractive, no larger than a man's fist. These, the hunters pointed out with respect as being among the most deadly killers in the forest.

Only once did Paul see a really massive creature during the day-time. It was a creature that the hunters called an ontholyn. It was furry, and fearsome, with tremendous clawed forepaws and a cavernous mouth. Paul watched it rear up on its hind legs to pick carefully of some fruit hanging at the top of a tall tree. It made a strange sound, half roaring and half trumpeting, then it sat back on its haunches to nibble the fruit. The sound, which had reverberated through the forest was, so the hunters said, merely an expression of pleasure. They claimed that the ontholyn was so slow that it was possible for a nimble man to run up to one, climb up its furry sides, tweak its nose and climb down again before the creature realized what was happening.

As the barge sped further away from Baya Nor along the Canal of Life, it seemed to Paul that he and his companions were making a journey back in time. The clusters of giant ferns, the bright orchidaceous flowers, the stringy lianas that now laced overhead from bank to bank of the canal, the tall, sad and utterly lethal Weeping Trees which leaked a tough, quick bonding and poisonous glue down their trunks to trap and kill small animals that would then putrefy and feed the exposed roots of the tree—all these conspired to make him feel that he was riding down a green tunnel into pre-history.

And, in fact, he was now riding through a green tunnel; for the banks of the Canal of Life had narrowed considerably. The foliage had closed in overhead, and sunlight was visible only as a dazzling maze of thin gold bars through which the barge seemed to cut its way with miraculous and hyp-notic ease.

As the light died, and the green gloom deepened, Shon Hu inspected the banks for a suitable place to moor the barge for the night.

"Lord," he said, "we have made good travel-ling. We are very near now to the Watering of Oruri."

"Would it not be good to journey on to the great river while we can still see?"

Shon Hu shrugged. "Who can say, lord? But my comrades like to see where they can plant their poles."

"That is very wise, Shon Hu. Therefore let us rest."

They found a small patch of ground near a group of the Weeping Trees. Shon Hu explained that most animals could smell the trees—particularly at night—and took great trouble to avoid them. That was why he had chosen the place. Neverthe-less, he advised that everyone should sleep in the barge.

The first night passed without incident. After

their evening meal the hunters began to exchange stories, as was their custom. Paul listened drowsily for a while, half drugged by the heavy night scents of the forest and the vapours rising from the water. The next thing he knew, it was daybreak — and a smiling Zu Shan was trying to tempt him with a handful of kappa and a strip of smoked meat that tasted like scorched rubber.

"You slept very soundly, Paul. We did not think you would take to the forest so well. How do your bones feel?" Zu Shan spoke in English, proud of the one distinction over the hunters that he possessed.

Paul groaned and tried to stretch. He groaned again—this time with much feeling. "I feel like an old man," he complained. "I feel as if the glue from the Weeping Trees had penetrated all my joints."

"It is the vapours from the water of the Canal of Life," explained Zu Shan. "They cause the bones to ache, but the pain passes away with vigorous movement. Poor Nemo feels it worst, I think, because his bones do not have their natural shape."

Little Nemo was crying like a baby. Paul picked him up and began to gently massage the twisted limbs. "Lord," gasped Nemo in Bayani, "you shame me. I beg of you, put me down."

Paul ruffled his hair affectionately and set him down in the stern of the barge. "It shall be as my son commands," he said gravely. "for I acknowledge before all present that you are truly my son."

"Lord," said Shon Hu, "there is much poling to be done. Will you speak the word?"

Paul raised his eyes to the steaming green roof overhead. Judging from the already oppressive atmosphere, it was going to be another hot and enervating day.

"Let us go, then," he said in Bayani, "with the blessing of Oruri."

## TWENTY-EIGHT

IT WAS ON THE SECOND night that disaster struck.

The Watering of Oruri was a broad, slow river, fairly shallow but easily navigable. Were it not for the mild current, the pole-men would have had an easier job propelling their craft up the river than along the Canal of Life.

To Paul, it seemed that there could be no end to this strange journey back in time—at least, not until they arrived at the very fount of creation. Baya Nor was less than two days travel away; yet already it belonged to another world—a world that, fancifully, seemed as if it would not begin to exist until hundreds of millennia had passed.

It was strange, this sense of journeying back in time. He had experienced the same sort of sensations in the donjons of Baya Nor and in the temple when Enka Ne had granted him his life but had commanded that each of his little fingers be struck off.

In a sense, perhaps, he really had journeyed back in time; for he had left the twenty-first century on Earth to travel many light-years and enter a medieval society on the 'far side of the sky'. But now, as he and his companions propelled themselves up a great musky river, flanked by high green walls of overpowering vegetation, even Baya Nor seemed ultra-modern.

The world he was in now seemed as if it had yet to experience the intrusion of man. The voyagers in their frail craft were nothing more than insubstantial dreams of the future, flitting like brief shadows through the long morning of pre-history.

They made camp for the night close by a mossy patch of ground that seemed both incongruous and refreshingly peaceful in the surrounding riot of green.

Life was lived at such a primitive and furious level in the forest through which the Watering of Oruri passed that Paul thought he could actually see plants growing. Oddly enough, although the trees and tree-ferns were much taller here than in the stretches of forest on each side of the Canal of Life, the gloom was not quite so unrelieved. Here and there, broad shafts of dying sunlight broke through the great green roof of foliage to create an odd impression of stained glass illumination in an endless green cathedral.

As he gazed idly at the river bank, tiny flowers closed their petals and almost shrank into the ground as if they were unwilling to witness the dark happenings of the long forest night.

Again the small band of explorers slept in their barge. As on the previous night, the hunters exchanged their stories—which, thought Paul, had much in common with the traditional anecdotes of fishermen back on Earth. He was less sleepy this time and managed to stay awake until one of the hunters took the first spell of the night watch. Then, with the sweeper rifle ready in his hand, he drifted luxuriously into a dark dimension of dreams that seemed strangely attuned to this world of pre-history.

It took several vital seconds for him, when the tragedy happened, to force himself back into consciousness. At first, the cries and the roars and the stench seemed to be part of the dream; but then the barge received a mighty blow and lurched violently. Paul rolled over, realized that he was awake and that the pandemonium was real.

He groped desperately for the sweeper rifle. Fitted along its barrel was a small atomic-powered pencil-beam torch, set parallel with the sights. It was his only source of light. Until he could find it and operate it, he could not possibly discover what was happening. The stench was terrible; but the screams were indescribable.

Frantically, he groped for the rifle. A century seemed to pass before he found it. He felt for the torch button and pressed it as he swung the rifle towards the sound of screaming.

The thin beam of intense light did not illuminate a wide area; but it revealed enough to turn his stomach to jelly.

There, on the bank of the river, was the largest and most terrible creature he had ever seen. As large, perhaps, as the prehistoric *Tyrannosaurus rex* of Earth, and certainly no less terrible.

He swung the torch beam up towards the massive and nightmarish head—then almost dropped the rifle in sheer terror. The head, arms and shoulders of one of the hunters protruded from a cavernous mouth.

Instantly, Paul swung the rifle away from the head, down the great curved back to where he judged the creature's belly must be. He pressed the trigger. Blue light shot through the darkness, parallel to the white light of the torch.

Added to the stench of the monster itself there was now the stench of its burning flesh. The fantastic creature seemed to be more surprised than hurt. With a casual and strangely delicate movement, it raised a great forearm and plucked the hunter from its mouth, flinging the body far out into the Watering of Oruri.

Then, with an almost comical calmness, it began to contemplate the unusual phenomenon of the blue and white beams of light. By that time the creature's stomach was burning, with the flesh sizzling and spitting. Gouts of flaming body fat fell to the ground; and smoky yellow flames curled up the high, scaly back.

The beast, thought Paul, hysterically, was already dead—but it just didn't know when to lie down. It stood there, watching itself being consumed by atomic fire as if the event were interesting but not altogether disturbing. Surely the blood must be boiling in its brain!

The whole scene appeared to drift into night-marish slow motion. Paul, hypnotized, could not take his eyes from the beast to see what his companions were doing. He continued pouring fantastic quantities of energy into the hide of a monster that seemed to have erupted from the very dawn of life.

At last, the terrible creature—almost burnt in two—appeared to realize that it was doomed. It shuddered, and the ground shuddered with it, then it gave a piercing scream—literally breathing fire, as burning flesh and air were expelled from its lungs, and rolled over, taking a tree with it. The thud of its body shook the bank, the barge and even the river. It must have been dead before it hit the ground.

Paul managed to pull himself together sufficiently to take his finger off the trigger of the sweeper rifle. But darkness did not descend, for the corpse of the beast had become a blazing inferno. The smell and the sounds were overpowering.

Shon Hu spoke the first coherent words. "Lord," he gasped with difficulty, "forgive me. I vomit."

He hung over the side of the barge and was joined within seconds by everyone except Nemo, who had curled himself up into a tight foetal ball and was unconscious.

"Who had died?" whispered Paul, when he could trust himself to speak once more.

"Mien She, lord. He was the one who watched. Perhaps the beast saw him move."

"Why did he not see the beast move? Or hear it?

Such a creature could not move without warning of its coming.''

"Lord, I know not. He is dead now. Let us not question his alertness, for he has suffered much, and it may be that his spirit would be sad to know that we doubted him.''

Paul glanced at the burning corpse once more, and was immediately sick again. When he had recovered, he said "How call you this monster?''

"Lord, it has no name," said Shon Hu simply. "We have not seen its like before. We do not wish to see its like again.''

"Let us go quickly from this place," said Paul, retching, "before we vomit ourselves to death. In future, two men will always watch, for it is clear that one may nod. Let us go quickly, now.''

"Lord, it is dark and we do not know the river.''

"Nevertheless, we will go.'' He gestured towards the still burning body. "Here is too much light—and other things. Come. I will take the pole of Mien She.''

## TWENTY-NINE

THERE WAS NOT A BREATH of wind. The forest was immensely quiet. Indeed, but for the dark green smells of night, it would have been possible to imagine that the forest had ceased to exist. Only the river seemed alive, murmuring sleepily as if it, too, wished to sink into a state of unbeing.

It had been a hard and dismal day—hard because the Watering of Oruri had narrowed, making the current more swift, and dismal because the death of Mien She was still very much on everyone's minds.

Nemo had been the worst affected. He had been the worst affected not only because he was a child but because he had experienced telepathically the brief but terrifying agony of Mien She. All day the crippled child had lain curled up at the stern of the bridge. He would not eat or even drink; and it was only by patient coaxing that Paul managed to get him to take a few mouthfuls of water at the evening meal.

There had been no cheerful exchange of tall stories when the hunters took their ease after a hard day's poling. When they spoke—if they spoke—it was almost monosyllabically and only because the communication was necessary.

Paul and Shon Hu had taken the first watch. Now they were also taking the last watch. Presently grey wisps of light would filter through the tall trees. Today they would leave the barge behind. Already they were in Lokhali country, and therefore the dangers were doubled. But, thought Paul, after the horror of the previous night, any brush with the Lokhali would seem by contrast to be a form of light relief.

As he sat back to back with Shon Hu, Paul realized that there was something concerning the Lokhali that was trying to surface in his conscious mind. Something important. Something that he had seen but not noticed . . .

His only encounter so far with the forest tribe had been at the mass crucifixion on the Fourth Avenue of the Gods. His mind flew back to that day and he could see again and hear again the dying Lokhali who, in his extreme agony, had murmured meaningless—and, in the circumstances, bizarre—fragments of German, French and English.

Suddenly, Paul realized what he had seen but not noticed. Four fingers and a thumb! The Lokhali were not only taller than the Bayani, but more perfectly formed. Four fingers and a thumb! Then his mind leaped back to the woman who bore her child near the kappa fields, and then to Mylai Tui, who had been angry at his questions and had then demanded to be chastized for displaying her anger.

And now here he was in the middle of a primeval forest, journeying in search of a legend and with a headful of unanswered questions. He wanted to laugh aloud. He wanted to laugh at the sheer absurdity, the incongruity of it all.

He did laugh aloud.

Shon Hu started. "You are amused, lord?" he asked reproachfully.

"Not really Shon Hu. I am sorry to startle you. I was just thinking of some things that Poul Mer Lo, the teacher, finds hard to understand."

"What manner of things, lord?"

Remembering the reactions of Mylai Tui, Paul thought carefully. "Shon Hu," he began, "we have not known each other long, but this venture joins us. You are my friend and brother."

"I am proud to be the friend of Poul Mer Lo. To become as his brother would do me too much honour."

"Nevertheless, my friend and brother, it is so. Therefore I do not wish to offend you."

Shon Hu was puzzled. "How can you offend me, lord, who have raised me in my own eyes?"

"By asking questions, Shon Hu. Only by asking questions."

"Lord, I see you wish to speak. Where no offence is offered none shall be taken."

"The questions concern the number of fingers a man should have, Shon Hu."

Immediately, Paul felt the hunter stiffen.

"Lord," said Shon Hu at length, "are there not certain things in your country of which it is very shameful to speak?"

Paul considered for a moment. "Yes, my friend, I think there are."

"So it is also with the Bayani. I tell you this, lord, so that you will understand if I do not find it easy to talk about the number of fingers a man should have. We have a saying: it is a thing that should be heard once and told once . . . Remember this, lord. Now ask the questions."

"Shon Hu, were you born with four fingers and a thumb, or with three?"

The hunter held up his hand. "See, lord." There were three fingers and a thumb.

Paul held up his own hand. "You have not answered the question. Look . . . But I was born with four fingers and a thumb—were you?"

"Lord, I—I do not know," said Shon Hu desperately.

"Are you sure? Are you sure you do not know?"

Shon Hu gulped. "Lord, I was told once by my father when he was dying that the left hand had been—defiled . . . But, it was such a little finger, lord, and the shame was easily remedied . . . This none living know, save you."

Paul smiled. "Be easy, my friend. None living, save me, shall ever know . . . I wonder how many more Bayani have been born imperfect?"

"I do not know. Not many, I think. The priests take those who are discovered. They are not seen again."

"Why is it so terrible to have four fingers?"

"Because, lord, those who have four fingers are the forsaken of Oruri. He smiles upon them not."

"Do you believe this?"

"Lord," said the hunter in an agitated voice, "I *must* believe. It is the truth."

"But why is it the truth?" asked Paul relentlessly.

"Lord, I can tell you only what I know . . . It is said that many many years ago, before there was a god-king in Baya Nor, the Bayani were not one people. There were those who were tall and lighter of skin, possessing four fingers and a thumb upon each hand. They were not, however, so numerous as the true Bayani, smaller, quicker of mind and body, possessing three fingers and a thumb upon each hand . . . There was much bloodshed, lord. Always there was much bloodshed. The tall ones with two fives believed themselves to be superior to the small ones with two fours. They ill-used the women of the fours. The fours retaliated and ill-used the women of the fives. Presently, there was a third warring faction—a number of outcasts with three fingers and a thumb on one hand and four fingers and a thumb on the other. Even among these people there was strife, since those with four fingers and a thumb on the right hand believed themselves to be superior to those with four fingers and a thumb on the left. And so the bloodshed became greater and more fierce, as each group reasoned that it alone was of the true blood and therefore most fitted to lead the rest."

"My friend," said Paul, "there is nothing new under the sun. In the story of my own people there has been much needless and futile strife."

"The war of the fingers reaches to the other side of the sky, then?" asked Shon Hu in surprise.

"No," said Paul, "the people of my own race are fortunate enough to possess the same number of fingers. So they found different reasons to inflict death and cruelty. They fought among themslves because some asserted that one particular god was greater than all other gods, or that one particular way of life was greater than all other ways of life, or that a white skin was better than a dark skin."

Shon Hu laughed. "Truly, your people, though great in strange skills must have been very simple of heart."

"Perhaps no less simple than the Bayani," retorted Paul gravely. "Proceed with your story, Shon Hu."

The hunter seemed, now, to be more relaxed. "Lord, it came to pass that there was seen more anger among the Bayani than there was love. Also, there was much fear. The crops were not tended because it was dangerous to go alone into the fields. The hunters found more profitable employment as hunters of men. Women prayed that their wombs might bear no fruit, for they were afraid to count the number of fingers on the hands of the babies they might bring forth. Few people died of great age, many died violently. And in time the number of the Bayani shrank, for the number of those who died became greater than the number of those who were born. It was clear that Oruri was displeased and that unless he could be brought to smile again, the people of the Bayani would be no more."

Paul sighed. "And all this because of the number of fingers on a man's hand."

"All this," repeated Shon Hu, "because of the number of fingers on a man's hand . . . But an answer was found, lord. It was found by the first oracle, who fasted unto the point of death, then spoke with the voice of Oruri. And the voice said: 'There shall come a man among you, who yet has no power and whose power will be absolute. And because no man may wield such power, the man shall be as a king. And because none may live for ever, the king shall be as a god. Each year the king must die that the god may be reborn.' This the priests of Oruri heard, and the words were good. So they approached the oracle and said: 'This surely is our salvation. How, then, may we recognize him who will take the form of a god?' To which the oracle replied: 'You shall not see his face, but you shall see his beak. You shall not see his hands, but you shall see his plumage. And you shall hear only the cry of a bird that has never flown.' "

To Paul Marlowe the story was fascinating, not only because it explained so much but because of its curious similarity in places to some of the ancient myths of Earth. "How was the first god-king revealed, Shon Hu?" he asked quietly.

"Lord, the priests could not understand the oracle, and the oracle would speak no more. But after many days, the thing came to pass. A priest of the Order of the Blind Ones—who then did not wear a hood, for they had yet to look upon the face

of the god-king—was going out to the kappa fields
when he saw a great bird covered in brilliant plumage. The bird was uttering the gathering call of the
Milanyl birds which, though birds of prey, were
nevertheless good to eat . . . But, lord, this Milanyl
bird had the legs of a man. It was a poor hunter
named Enka Ne, who, too weak with hunger to
hunt as a man, sought to entice game in this manner.''

''And this, then, was the god-king.''

''Yes, lord, Enka Ne was truly the god-king. For
he was granted the wisdom of Oruri. On the day
that he was shown to the people, he gathered many
hunters about him. Then he took off his plumage
before the Bayani for the first and last time. He
held out his hands. And the people saw that on one
there was three fingers and a thumb and on the
other four fingers and a thumb. Then, in a loud
voice, Enka Ne said: 'It is fitting that there should
be an end to destruction among us. It is fitting,
also, that the hands of a man should be as the
hands of his brother. But a man cannot add to the
number of his fingers. Therefore let him rejoice
that he can yet take away.' Then he held out his
right hand and commanded a hunter to strike off
the small finger. And he said to the people: 'Let all
who remain in this land number their fingers as is
the number of my fingers. Happy are they whose
fingers are already thus. Happier still are they who
can make a gift of their flesh to Oruri. Wretched are
they who do not give when the gift is required. Let
them go from the land for ever, for there can be no
peace between us.' When Enka Ne had spoken,
many people held out their hands to the hunters.

But there was also much fighting. In the end, those who refused to give were either slaughtered or driven away."

Patches of light were beginning to show through the treetops. The last watch of the night was over. Paul stood up and stretched himself. Suddenly he was pleased with himself. He felt that he had found a missing piece of the puzzle.

"That was a very wonderful story, Shon Hu," he said at length.

"It is also a terrible story, lord," said Shon Hu. "I have spoken it once. I must not speak it again. As you have discovered, the shadow of the fingers still lies over Baya Nor; and blood continues to be spilled even after many years. The god-kings have never loved those with too much knowledge of this thing. Nor do they love those who, contrary to the desire of Oruri, are born with too many fingers." Shon Hu also stood up and stretched.

"I see . . . I am grateful that you have told me these things, Shon Hu. Let us speak now of the Lokhali."

"There is a Lokhali village," said the hunter, "perhaps the largest, near the bank of the river no more than a few hours of poling from here. Fortunately, we may leave the Watering of Oruri and strike through the forest before we reach it."

"Do the Lokhali have barges, Shon Hu?"

"Yes, lord, but their barges are very poor and very small. They only use the river when they are in great need. For they are much afraid of water."

"Then surely it is safer to voyage past their village in the water than to pass through the forest?"

"Lord, it may be so. But a man does not care to come near to the Lokhali."

"Nevertheless, I would pass the village . . . I think I know why the Bayani and the Lokhali have hated and feared each other for many years. The word Lokhali means accursed, wretched, cast out—does it not?"

"That is so, lord."

"And the Lokhali," went on Paul relentlessly, "do not appear to find four fingers and a thumb offensive . . . It seems to me, Shon Hu, that the Lokhali and Bayani were once brothers."

# THIRTY

COMPARED TO THE CITY OF Baya Nor, the Lokhali village was a miserable affair. There was only one great hall, or temple, of stone. The rest of the buildings—though many of them were reasonably large—were of mud bricks, wooden frames, and thatch. Many of the bricks were decorated with pieces of flint that had probably been pressed into them while they were still wet.

All this Paul noticed as the barge passed the village, keeping well to the far side of the Watering of Oruri, out of the range of spears and darts.

In fact, if size were any criterion, the village could more properly be called a town; for though the houses were primitive there were many of them and they had been carefully arranged with a certain amount of symmetry.

It was mid-morning, and a great many of the Lokhali were about, including a few dozen womenfolk at the water's edge, some washing and bathing while others were apparently cleaning food, utensils and even children. Those who were actually in the river scrambled rapidly ashore at the approach of the barge. Their cries brought more people down from the village, as well as a party of warriors or hunters. One or two of these roared and shook their weapons ferociously; but none seemed inclined to take to the few small, unstable-looking canoes that lay on the bank.

Paul realized the hopelessness of trying to find out anything of the rest of the crew of the *Gloria Mundi*. From that distance it would have been impossible to distinguish between European and Lokhali—unless the Europeans were wearing their own clothes. And as he himself had, of necessity, long ago taken to Bayani costume, it seemed reasonably certain that any survivors of the star ship would similarly have adopted the brief Lokhali garments.

It was tantalizing to be so near to a possible source of information and yet to be able to do nothing about it. But was there really nothing at all he could do? He thought carefully for a moment or two. Then he picked up his sweeper rifle and aimed at the water about twenty metres from the line of Lokhali on the bank. He pressed the trigger.

The rifle vibrated, producing its faint whine, then a patch of water began to hiss and bubble until it produced a most impressive waterspout. There were cries of awe and consternation from the Lokhali on the bank. Some ran away or drew back, but

most seemed almost hypnotized by the phenomenon.

The display would serve two purposes, thought
Paul with satisfaction. It would discourage the
Lokhali, perhaps, from following the barge along
the bank while at the same time the demonstration
of such power—or the news of it—would convey
to any surviving Europeans that there was yet
another survivor.

He put down the rifle then cupped his hands
round his mouth and shouted loudly across the
water: "I will come again . . . *Je reviens . . . Ich
komm wieder.*"

Soon the barge was well past the village. Paul
continued to gaze back intently until the river bent
slightly and the Lokhali village was out of sight.

Shortly before the sun had reached its zenith,
Shon Hu selected a suitable spot on the river bank
and guided the barge in towards it.

"We must now pass through the forest, lord,"
he said. "To travel further along the Watering of
Oruri would only increase the journey."

"Then let us eat and rest," said Paul. "Afterwards we will divide that which we have brought
into packs that a man may carry."

When they had eaten and rested, they took the
water skins, the dried kappa, the smoked strips of
meat, the skins they had brought to protect themselves in the cold uplands, and the sling that had
been made for Nemo, out of the barge. Then they
deliberately capsized it and weighted it down to
the river bed with heavy stones. It was, perhaps,
unlikely that the Lokhali would discover the
barge, anyway; but if it were submerged, there

would be even less chance. The only real problem, thought Paul grimly, would be in finding it themselves when they returned from the Temple of the White Darkness. It was true that they could get back to Baya Nor without the barge, but the journey would be considerably harder—and more dangerous.

As the afternoon shadows lengthened, the group moved away from the Watering of Oruri with Shon Hu in the lead. Paul followed immediately behind him, and after Paul came Zu Shan with Nemo slung like an awkward child from his back. The rearguard consisted of the two remaining hunters.

Remarkably enough, Nemo seemed to have almost completely recovered from the death of Mien She. But Paul noticed that at all times he stayed very close to Zu Shan. The two had come to depend on each other. Though Zu Shan was half a man, he was also still only half a boy. Basically, he found much more satisfaction talking to Nemo than to Paul or the hunters.

The two of them liked to demonstrate their assumed superiority over the Bayani by jabbering away to each other in English; interlaced with a few Bayani words and phrases. The resulting medley was very odd and, at times, amusing. It brought the boys closer and closer together. Originally, the plan had been that everyone should take turns in carrying Nemo. But this neither Nemo nor Zu Shan would permit. Fortunately, Nemo, being hardly more than a small bundle of skin and bone himself, was no heavier—and probably not quite as heavy—as the bundles that the rest, including Paul, were carrying.

Despite the fact that the group had to travel slowly, and somewhat noisily—if the pained expression on Shon Hu's face was any indication—along the perimeter of what was clearly regarded by the Bayani as Lokhali country, the fierce warriors of the forest were never seen. Nor, surprisingly enough, were many wild animals. Perhaps it was as Shon Hu claimed—that the great noise of their passing was sufficient to send any wild things other than belligerent carnivores far out of range of the intruders.

Whatever the reason, they passed two nights and the best part of three days safely in the forest—the only disturbing incident being when a tree-snake fell on Paul. But the small, fearsome-looking creature seemed quite as shaken by the encounter as he was, and rapidly disappeared.

The forest did not end abruptly. It simply began to thin out, so that the leaves of the trees no longer created an interwoven roof that shut out the sky. Paul noticed that the ground became more firm and less damp. The air was growing cooler, and it became obvious that the ground ahead was rising slowly. Presently, large patches of blue became noticeable between the tree-tops. Paul realized then how much he had been missing the open sky.

The forest gave way to savannah—rich grassland where the trees were few and scattered and were often no higher than the grass itself, which frequently came up to the shoulders of the small Bayani. Far ahead, Paul could see the uplands. Beyond them, now and again becoming briefly visible in the haze of late afternoon, there seemed to be a shimmering range of white-tipped mountains. Was it a trick of his imagination or was there really one that stood far higher than the rest? One that he knew instinctively was the Temple of the White Darkness.

Shortly before the sun set, they made camp in the middle of the rolling savannah. Now that the forest was behind, making the death of Mien She seem oddly remote, now that it was possible to see the stars and the nine sisters—the nine moons of Altair Five—once more, the spirits of the hunters rose. After their evening meal, they wrapped themselves in skins against the cool night air and told stories to each other as before.

Paul had hoped that it would have been possible to make a fire. But to have started a fire in the middle of the savannah would have been very dangerous indeed—besides which, it would have been difficult to find sufficient fuel for one. So he was content to lean against his pillow of skins, himself warmly wrapped and listen vaguely to the chattering of the Bayani.

As he gazed idly at the stars, he began to think. In the journey through the forest—a timeless journey through time—he had apparently cast off the personality and conditioning of Poul Mer Lo. For some reason he could not understand, in some way he could not understand, he had become very consciously Paul Marlowe, native of Earth, once more.

And the surprising thing was that it no longer hurt. He was a castaway, far from home, and with no hope of returning. Yet, it no longer hurt . . .

He was amazed at the discovery.

Presently, the talk of the hunters died down and

they made ready for sleep. Zu Shan and Nemo were already asleep, having tired themselves out with the day's journey. Presently, Paul and Shon Hu shared the first watch.

They did not talk. Shon Hu, though satisfied with the day's progress and relieved now that the forest was behind them, was not inclined to be very communicative. This suited Paul who was able—pleasurably for once—to contemplate the night sky and let his thoughts drift among the stars.

When it was time to wake the two hunters for their spell of watch, Paul felt more exhilarated than tired. Perhaps it was the effect of the cooler, bracing air. Or perhaps it was because they were nearing the end of the journey.

Nevertheless he very quickly fell asleep when at last he lay down.

# THIRTY-ONE

HE WAS AWARE OF WORDS BEING spoken loudly
and urgently in his head. Vaguely and sleepily he
tried to dismiss them as some aspect of a dream
that he was not aware of dreaming. But the words
would not be dismissed. They were not to be
abolished either by sleepiness or will-power. They
would not be ignored. They became louder, more
insistent.

Until he sat bolt upright, listening to them with a
sensation of panic that it was hard to fight down. In
the starlight, he could see dimly that the others
were also sitting upright. They, too were
listening—motionless, as if the sound that was not
a sound had frozen the living flesh. There was also
another sound—a real sound—that seemed very

far away. With an effort, Paul concentrated on it. With an even greater effort, he managed to analyse it—the sound of Nemo whimpering. Then his thoughts were snapped back by the loud, imperative and utterly soundless message.

*"If you would live to a ripeness, go back!*
*If you would toil in the fields,*
*if you would hunt in the forest,*
*if you would rest in the evening, go back.*
*If you would look upon women and beget children,*
*if you would discourse with brothers and fathers,*
*if you would gather the harvest of living,*
*if you would pass your days in contentment,*
*having heard the voice of Aru Re,*
*go back! Go back! Go back!"*

The words without sound became silent. No one moved.

Shon Hu was the first to speak. "Lord," he said shakily, "we have heard the voice of Oruri and still live. This journey is not favoured. Now must we return."

Paul tried desperately to marshal his racing thoughts. "The voice spoke to you in Bayani, Shon Hu?"

"Most clearly, lord."

"And yet it spoke to me in English—the language of my own country."

"Such is the mystery of Oruri."

"Not Oruri," said Paul positively, "but *Aru Re*."

"Paul," said Zu Shan, "the voice spoke to me in both English and Bayani."

Paul was silent for a moment. Then he said in English: "That, I suppose, is because you are now able to think in both languages . . . What about you, Nemo? Are you all right?"

Nemo's whimpering had stopped. "I am very much afraid," he confessed in a thin, high voice. "I—I cannot remember what language I heard."

Paul tried to laugh and ease the tension. "You are not alone, Nemo. We were all very much afraid."

"We shall go back to Baya Nor, then?" The child's voice was pleading.

Paul considered for a moment, wondering if he had any right to ask his companions to go further. But how tantalizing, how heart-breaking to be so near and to have to turn back.

At length he spoke in Bayani. "Already, I have asked too much of my friends and brothers," he said. "We have faced danger, one of us has died and there is, doubtless, much danger still to be faced. I cannot ask more of those who have already shown great courage . . . Any who wish now to return, having heard what they have heard, will go with my thoughts and prayers, As for me, Shon Hu has fulfilled that which I asked. He has shown me the way. Doubtless, I shall reach the Temple of the White Darkness, if Oruri so desires. I have spoken."

"Lord," said Shon Hu, "truly greatness sits upon you. A man cannot die in better company. This, perhaps, Oruri will consider when the time comes. I will go with you."

There was a short silence, then one of the two remaining hunters spoke: "We are ashamed in the presence of Poul Mer Lo and Shon Hu. Formerly, we were brave men. Forgive us, lord . . . For some, it seems there is no end to courage. For others, the end comes quickly.''

"My brothers," said Paul, "courage has many faces. I count myself fortunate that I have travelled this far with you . . . Go when the first light comes, and a man may see the way ahead. Also, take with you Zu Shan and Nemo; for I rejoice in the knowledge that you will bring them safely to Baya Nor.''

"Lord," said Zu Shan in Bayani, "the gift of Enka Ne remains with him to whom the gift was made . . . I think, also, the little one may desire to stay.''

Nemo seemed to have recovered himself. "The little one desires much," he said, also in Bayani, "but he will stay in the shadow of Poul Mer Lo.''

Shon Hu laughed grimly. "Thus are we a formidable company.''

"It is in such company," retorted Paul enigmatically, "that men may move mountains . . . Now listen to my thoughts. The voice, it seems, spoke to each of us in a different manner. To me it spoke in my tongue, calling itself *Aru Re*. To you, Shon Hu, it spoke in your tongue. And to Zu Shan in a mixture of my tongue and his. But the message was the same for all of us, I think . . . Zu Shan, what did you understand by the message?''

"That we should not go forward, otherwise we should die.''

"Ah," said Paul triumphantly, "but that was not what the voice said. It advised us, *if we desired certain things*, to go back. It advised, Zu Shan. It did not command. It advised us—if we desired security, long life, contentment, peace of mind— to return the way we came. But the voice did not advise us what to do if we desired knowledge, did it?"

There was a silence. Eventually, Shon Hu said: "Lord, there is much mystery in your words. I do not understand where your thoughts lead, but I have made my decision and I will follow."

"What I am trying to say," explained Paul patiently, "is that I think the voice meant to turn us back only if we did not have the resolution and the curiosity to go forward."

"When Oruri speaks," said Shon Hu with resignation, "who dare question the meaning?"

"But when *Aru Re* speaks in English," said Paul, emphasizing the separate words, "the meaning must be sought more carefully."

"Lord," said one of the hunters who were returning to Baya Nor, "we shall not take the barge. We shall leave it in the hope that Poul Mer Lo—who has wrought many wonders—will require it yet again."

## THIRTY- TWO

THERE WERE NO MORE voices in the dark. Nor did
Oruri—or *Aru Re*—utter his soundless words in
the daytime. After less than a day's travel, Paul
noticed that the long savannah grass was getting
shorter. Presently it was only as high as his knee.
Presently, no higher than his ankle. The air grew
colder as they came to the uplands.

And there before them, less than half a day's
march away, was the mountain range whose central peak was called the Temple of the White Darkness. All that lay between was a stretch of scrub-
land, rising into moorland and small patches of
coniferous forest.

Suddenly, Paul became depressed. Through the
high, clear air, he could see the detail of the jagged
rock-face of the mountain—capped and scarred
by everlasting snow. And sweeping round the base
of the mountain was a great glacier—a broad river
of ice whose movement could probably be
reckoned in metres per year.

As they made their last camp before they came to the mountain, there were distant muted rumbles, as if the mountain were aware of their presence and resented their approach. The three Bayani—the man, the youth and the child—had never heard the sound of avalanches before.

Paul had much difficulty explaining the phenomenon to them. Eventually, he gave it up, seeing that they could not clearly understand. To them, the noise was only one more manifestation of the displeasure of Oruri.

He gazed despairingly at the Temple of the White Darkness, wondering how he could possibly begin his search. He was no mountaineer. Nor was he equipped for mountaineering. And it would be sheer cruelty to drag his companions—children of the forest—across the dangerous slopes of ice and snow. How terrible it was to be so near and yet so helpless. For the first time he was ready to acknowledge to himself the probability of defeat.

Then the sunset came—and with it a sign. Paul Marlowe was not easily moved to prayer. But, on this occasion, prayer was not just the only thing he was able to offer. It seemed strangely appropriate and even inevitable.

There, far above the moorland and the ring of coniferous forest, as the sun sank low, he saw briefly a great curving stem of fire.

He had seen something similar many, many years ago in a world on the other side of the sky. As he watched, and as the sun sank and the stem of the fire dissolved, he remembered how it had been when he first saw sunlight reflected from the polished hull of the *Gloria Mundi*.

# THIRTY-THREE

PAUL MARLOWE WAS alone. He had left his companions on the far side of the glacier. Shon Hu was partly snow blind, Zu Shan's nose had started to bleed because of the altitude, and little Nemo, wrapped in skins so that he looked like a furry ball, had an almost perpetual aching in his bones.

So Paul had left the three of them on the far side of the glacier and had set off alone shortly after dawn. He had told them that, if he had not returned by noon, they must go without waiting for him. He did not think that they could stand another night on the bare, lower slopes of the mountain.

The glacier had looked much more formidable than it really was. His feet and ankles ached a great deal with the effort of maintaining footholds on the great, tilting ice sheets; and from the way his toes felt it seemed as if sharp slivers of ice might have cut through the tough skins that were his only protection. But on the whole, apart from being bruised by innumerable minor falls, he felt he was in reasonable shape.

And now, here he was, standing near the base of one of the mighty metal shoes that supported the three impossibly slender legs of the great star ship. The shoes rested firmly on a broad flat table of rock in the lee of the mountain, and they were covered to a depth of perhaps three metres by eternal ice. The legs themselves were easily twenty metres tall; and the massive hull of the star ship rose all of two hundred metres above them—like a spire. Like the spire of a vast, buried cathedral.

Paul gazed up at the fantastic shape, shielding his eyes against the glow of its polished surface, and was drunk with wonder.

Then the voice that was no voice spoke in his head.

"I am beautiful, am I not?"

So much had happened that Paul was beyond surprise. He said calmly: "Yes, you are beautiful."

"I am *Aru Re*—in your language, Bird of Mars. I have waited here more than fifty thousand planetary years. It may be that I shall wait another ten thousand years before my children are of an age to understand. For I am the custodian of the memory of their race."

Suddenly, Paul's mind was reeling. Here he was, a man of Earth, having made a hazardous journey on a strange planet, through primeval forests, across wide savannah, into the mountains and over a high glacier to meet a telepathic star ship. A star ship that spoke in English, called itself the Bird of Mars and claimed to have been in existence for over fifty thousand years. He wanted to laugh and cry and quietly and purposefully go mad. But there was no need of that. Obviously he was already mad. Obviously, the glacier had beaten him and he was lying now—what was left of him—in some shallow crevasse, withdrawn into a world of fantasy, waiting for the great cold to bring down the final curtain on his psychic drama.

"No, you are not mad," said the silent voice. "Nor are you injured and dying. You are Paul Marlowe of Earth, and you are the first man resolute enough to discover the truth. Open your mind completely to me, and I will show you much that has been hidden. I am *Aru Re*, Bird of Mars... The truth also, is beautiful."

"Nothing but a machine!" shouted Paul, rebelling against the impossible reality. "You are nothing but a machine—a sky-high lump of steel, wrapped round a computer with built-in paranoia." He tried to control himself, but could not restrain the sobbing. "Fraud! Impostor! Bastard lump of tin!"

"Yes, I am a machine," returned the voice of the *Aru Re*, insistently in his head, "but I am greater than the sum of my parts. I am a machine that lives. Because I am the custodian and the carrier of the seed, I am immortal. I am greater than the men who conceived me, though they, too, were great."

"A machine!" babbled Paul desperately. "A useless bloody machine!"

The voice would not leave him alone. "And

what of Paul Marlowe, voyager in the *Gloria Mundi*, citizen on sufferance of Baya Nor, Poul Mer Lo, the teacher? Is he not a machine—a machine constructed of bone and flesh and dreams?"

"Leave me alone!" sobbed Paul. "Leave me alone!"

"I cannot leave you alone," said the *Aru Re*, "because you chose not to leave me alone. You chose to know. I warned you to go back, but you came on. Therefore, according to the design, you shall know. Open your mind completely."

Dimly, Paul knew that there was a battle raging in his head. He did not want to lose it. Because he knew instinctively that if he did lose it he would never be quite the same again.

"Open your mind," repeated the star ship.

With all his strength, Paul fought against the voice and the compulsive power that had invaded his brain.

"Then close your eyes and forget," murmured the *Aru Re* persuasively. "It has been a long journey. Close your eyes and forget."

The change of approach caught Paul Marlowe off guard. Momentarily, he closed his eyes; and for the fraction of a second he allowed the taughtness to slacken.

It was enough for the star ship. As great spirals of blackness whirled in upon him, he realized that he was in thrall.

There was no sensation of movement, but he was no longer on the Mountain of the White Darkness. He was in a black void—the most warm, the most pleasant, the most comfortable void in the universe.

And suddenly, there was light.

He looked up at (down upon? around?) the most beautiful city he had ever seen. It grew—blossomed would have been a better word—in a desert. The desert was not a terrestrial desert, and the city was not a terrestrial city, and the men and women who occupied it—brown and beautiful and human though they looked—were not of Earth.

"This city of Mars," said the *Aru Re*, "grew, withered and died before men walked upon Sol Three or Altair Five. This city, on the fourth planet of your sun, contained twenty million people and lasted longer than the span of the entire civilizations of Earth. By your standards it was stable—almost immortal. And yet it, too, died. It died as the whole of Mars died, in the Wars of the Great Cities that lasted two hundred and forty Martian years, destroying in the end not only a civilization but the life of the planet that gave it birth."

The scene changed rapidly. As Paul Marlowe looked, it seemed as if the city were expanding and contracting like some fantastic organism inhaling and exhaling, pulsing with life—and death. In the accelerated portrayal of Martian history that he was now witnessing, buildings and structures more than two kilometres high were raised and destroyed in the fraction of a second. Human beings were no longer visible, not even as a blur. Their time span was too short. And every few seconds the desert and the city would erupt briefly into the bright, blinding shapes that Paul recognized from pictures he had seen long ago—the terrible glory of transient mushrooms of atomic fire.

"Thus," went on the matter of fact voice of the *Aru Re*, "did Martian civilization encompass its own suicide . . . Think of a culture and a technology, Paul Marlowe, as far ahead of yours as yours is ahead of the Bayani. Think of it, and know that such a culture can still be vulnerable as men themselves are always vulnerable . . . But there were those—men and machines—who foresaw the end. They knew that the civilization of Mars, inherently unstable, would perish. Yet they knew also that, with the resources at their command, three hundred million years of Martian evolution need not be in vain."

The scene changed, darkened. Without knowing how he knew, Paul realized that he was now gazing at a large subterranean cavern, kilometres below the bleak Martian desert. Here other structures were growing, like strange and beautiful stalagmites, from the floor of living rock. Men and machines scuttled about them, ant-like, swarming. Everywhere there was a sense of urgency and purpose and speed.

"And so the star ships were built—the seed cases that would be cast off by a dying planet to carry the seeds of its achievement to the still unravaged soil of distant worlds . . . Here is the rocky bed where I and six other identical vessels were created. It would have been comparatively easy to build star ships that were no more than star ships. But we were created as guardians—living guardians, fashioned from materials almost impervious to the elements and even time itself. Our task was not only to transport, but to nurture and prepare the seed; and when the seed had again taken root, when the flower of civilization had begun to bloom again, it would be our task to restore the racial memory and reveal the origin of that which could now only achieve maturity on an alien soil. Many died that we might be programmed for life. Many remained behind that we might carry the few—the few who were to become as children, their minds cleansed of all sophistication and personal memories so that they might rediscover a lost innocence, learning once more over the long centuries of reawakening, the nature of their human predicament."

Again the scene accelerated. The star ships grew towards the roof of the cavern. In a silent, explosive puff, the roof itself was blasted away by some invisible force. Two of the star ships crumpled swiftly and soundlessly to lie like twisted strips of metal foil on the floor of a great rocky basin that was now open to the sky. A tiny, thin, blurred snake—that Paul Marlowe knew was a stream of human beings—rippled to the base of each of the remaining star ships. And was swallowed. Then, one by one, each of the silver vessels became shrouded by blue descending aureoles of light. The rock floor turned to brilliant liquid fire as the star ships lifted gracefully and swiftly into the black reaches of the sky.

"That was how the exodus took place," continued the *Aru Re*. "That was how the seed-cases carried the seed. Of the five ships that left Mars, one proceeded to Sirius Four, where a great civilization is now maturing; one voyaged to Alpha Centauri One, where the seed withered before it had taken root; another journeyed to Procyon

Two, where the seed remains still only the seed,
and where there is yet little distinction between
men and animals; the fourth vessel, myself, came
here to Altair Five, where, it seems, the flower
may yet blossom; and the last vessel made the
shortest voyage, to Sol Three, the planet you call
Earth. Its seed lived and flourished, though the
star ship was destroyed, having settled on land
that possessed a deep geological fault. It is now
more than nine millennia since the island on
which the star ship rested was submerged below
the waters you know as the Atlantic Ocean."

Paul's mind was numbed by revelations,
traumatized by knowledge, shattered by incredi-
ble possibilities. The Martian scene had faded, and
there was now nothing. He floated dreamily and
luxuriously in a sea of darkness, an intellectual
limbo in which it was only possible to assume
'sanity' by actually believing that these fantastic
experiences had been communicated to him by a
telepathic star ship.

"Your body grows cold," said the *Aru Re* in-
comprehensibly, "and there is little time left for
me to answer the questions that are boiling in your
mind. Soon I must allow you to return. But here
are some of the answers that you seek. It is true
that my mind is a linked series of what you would
call computers, but it also stores the implanted
patterns of the minds of men long dead. It bears no
more relation to what you understand by the term
computer than your *Gloria Mundi* bore to its ancestor, the guided missile. You wish to know how I
can speak your tongue and converse of the things
you have known. I can speak the language used by

any intelligent being by exploring its mind and correlating symbols and images. You wish to know also if I can still communicate with the remaining star ships, the guardians that await the maturation of their seed, as I do. We communicate not by any form of wave transmission that you can understand, but by elaborate patterns of empathy that are not subject to the limiting characteristics of space and time."

It seemed to Paul that, in the black silence of his head, there was a great drum roll of titanic laughter. "Is it so strange, little one," said the *Aru Re* softly and with irony, "that even a machine can grow lonely? Also, we need to share the knowledge when the first of the seed brings forth a truly mature fruit. For then there can be no doubt that the scattering of the seed was not in vain . . . I will answer one more question, and then you must return if you are to live. You are puzzled by the variation in the number of fingers of the race you have discovered. There was some small genetic damage during transit, which caused slight mutations. The variations are of no importance. It matters not in the long sweep of history." Again the titanic roll of laughter. "In the end, little one, despite their now rigid tabu of the little finger, the far descendants of the Bayani will be as their Martian ancestors were. But perhaps they will have out-lived the impulse to self-destruction . . . Now, farewell, Paul Marlowe. Your mind flickers and your body grows cold . . . *Open your eyes!*"

The darkness dissolved; and once more there was feeling—pain and exhaustion and extreme cold.

Paul opened his eyes. He was still standing at the base of one of the metal shoes of the star ship. Had he ever moved from it? He did not know. Perhaps he would never know. He stared about him, dazed, trance-like, trying to accept the realities of a real world once more.

The ache in his limbs helped to focus his mind on practicalities. His limbs were stiff and painful—as if they had been rigid a very long time, or as if he had just come out of suspended animation.

Shielding his eyes, he gazed up at the polished hull of the great star ship and then down at its supporting shoes embedded in eternal ice. That at least was real. He stood contemplating it for some moments.

Then he said softly: "Yes, you are truly beautiful."

He had told Shon Hu and the others not to wait for him after mid-day. The sun was already quite high in the sky. He felt weak and shattered; but there was no time to waste if he were to recross the glacier before they attempted to make their own way back to Baya Nor.

Then, suddenly, there was a curious rippling in his limbs—a glow, a warmth, as if liquid energy were being pumped into his veins. He felt stronger than he had ever felt. He could hardly keep still.

Impulsively, and for no apparent reason, he held out his arm—a strange half-gesture of gratitude and farewell—to the high, sun-bright column of metal that was the *Aru Re*.

Then he turned and set off on the journey back across the glacier.

. . .

Zu Shan saw him coming in the distance.

Shon Hu, partly snow blind, could hardly see anything.

Nemo did not need to see. His face wore an expression in which wonder mingled with something very near to ecstasy.

"Lord," he said in Bayani when Paul was only a few paces away, "I have been trying to ride your thoughts. There has never been such a strange ride. I fell off, and fell off, and fell off."

"I, too, fell off," said Paul, "perhaps even more than you did."

"You are all right, Paul?" asked Zu Shan anxiously in English.

"I don't think I have felt better for a long time," answered Paul honestly.

"Lord," said Shon Hu, "I cannot see your face, but I can hear your voice, and that shows me the expression on your face . . . I am happy that you have found what you have found . . . The little one told us many strange things, lord, which are much beyond the thinking of such men as I . . . It is true, then, that you have spoken with Oruri?"

"Yes, Shon Hu. I have spoken with Oruri. Now let us return from the land of gods to the land of men."

# THIRTY-FOUR

THERE WERE NOW only two experienced pole-men
to control the barge. But by this time Paul himself
had acquired some of the tricks and the rhythm of
poling, and he was able to relieve Shon Hu and Zu
Shan for reasonably long spells; while Nemo continued to nurse his still aching bones in the stern of
the small craft. Fortunately, navigation was not
too difficult for they were now passing down
stream. The poling was necessary as much to
guide the barge as to add to its speed.

The journey back from the Temple of the White
Darkness to the bank of the river had been easier
than Paul had expected. Perhaps it was psychologically easier because they were relieved because
the mountain had been reached without any

further disasters, and they were now going home. Or perhaps it was because they were already familiar with the hazards of the route and also because Shon Hu's uncanny sense of direction had enabled them to reach the Watering of Oruri less than a kilometre from where they had sunk the barge.

Shon Hu had completely recovered from his snow blindness by the time they had reached the savannah. As soon as they were on the lower ground, they made camp and rested for a day and a night before going back into the forest. They did not hear the voice of the *Aru Re* again—though, out of curiosity, Paul exercised what mental concentration he possessed in an attempt to contact it telepathically. It seemed as if the star ship had now dismissed them altogether from its lofty contemplations.

Though they had found the barge without too much difficulty, it took the three of them the best part of an afternoon to clear it of stones and sediment and refloat it. By that time they were tired out; and though there was still enough light left to pass the Lokhali village before darkness fell, Shon Hu judged it safer to wait until the following morning. By then the barge would have dried out and, with a full day's poling, they could be far from the Lokhali before they had to make a night camp once more.

So it was that shortly after dawn the barge drifted round a slight bend in the Watering of Oruri, and the Lokhali village came in sight. There were few people about this time—probably many of the Lokhali were still at their morning meal— but three or four men were sitting in a little group, desultorily fashioning what looked like spear shafts out of straight, slender pieces of wood. There were also some women bathing or washing. And one who stood apart from the rest and seemed neither to be bathing or washing, but watching.

Paul handed his pole back to Zu Shan and took up his sweeper rifle. At a distance of perhaps a hundred metres, he saw that there was something odd about the solitary woman. She was virtually naked as the rest were; and at that distance her skin seemed quite as dark as that of the others—but she had white hair. Everyone else had black hair. But this one, the solitary one, had white hair.

Paul cast his mind back desperately to the occupants of the *Gloria Mundi*. None of them had white hair. With the exception of the Swedish woman who had been—inevitably—blonde, all of them had been rather dark. And Ann—Ann's hair had been quite black.

But there was something about the solitary woman on the bank, now only sixty or seventy metres away . . .

Paul had long ago decided on a plan of action if there were any *Gloria Mundi* survivors, able to move freely, in the Lokhali village. It was an extremely simple plan, but his resources were such that it was impossible to risk anything elaborate like a direct assault. For the atomic charge in the sweeper rifle was now ominously low.

However, there were still three factors in his favour: he had some element of surprise, he had a strange and powerful weapon, and he knew that the Lokhali didn't like travelling on water.

Shon Hu and Zu Shan had already been warned

to keep the barge steady on command. Now, if only . . .

The Lokhali had seen the barge; but though the women had come out of the water and the men had picked up their spears, no one seemed inclined to try and do anything about it. They just stood and stared—sullenly and intently. The woman with the white hair seemed to be concentrating her attention on Paul, and on the weapon he held.

With little more than forty metres separating the barge from the bank, Paul judged that now, if at all, he must make the attempt. Probably there were no Europeans left. And even if there were, the chances of being able to contact them, quite apart from rescuing them, would be pretty remote.

And yet . . . and yet . . . And yet, the woman with the white hair seemed to be meeting his gaze. That slight movement of the arm—could it be a discreet signal?

*"Gloria Mundi!"* he shouted. *"Gloria Mundi!"* He raised the rifle and waved it. "Into the water—quick! *Venez ici! Kommen Sie hier!* I'll give covering fire!"

Suddenly, the woman with the white hair ran into the water, splashing and wading out to swimming depth. To Paul it seemed as if she were moving in horribly slow motion. But the miraculous thing was nobody looked like stopping her. Then a woman cried out and the spell was broken. A tall Lokhali swung his spear arm back, so did another. Then a third began to run after the woman with white hair. The water was not yet up to her waist, and she still did not have free swimming room.

"Hurry, damn you!" he shouted. "Hurry!"

He sighted the rifle carefully over her head, fixing on the patch of water between her and the bank. He pressed the trigger.

The rifle whined feebly, faintly; and the water began to hiss and steam. The Lokhali who had tried to follow stopped dead. The two with spears ran towards him. The woman was already able to swim, and the bubbling water behind her had now turned into a water spout—effectively deterring pursuit and partly screening her from the men on the bank.

Then the sweeper rifle died. Its atomic charge had finally reached equilibrium.

The water spout subsided. All that was left to deter the Lokhali was a patch of very warm water—rapidly being carried downstream by the current—and a condensing cloud of steam.

One of the Lokhali hurled a spear. It fell almost exactly between the woman and the barge. By that time, she was less than twenty metres away from it, but she was making very slow progress and seemed curiously tired.

If Paul had stopped to think then, the tragedy might possibly have been averted. It did not occur to him until later that the spear might have been hurled not at the woman but at the barge.

But, without thinking, he flung the useless rifle down and dived into the water, hoping at least to create a diversion. It was not the diversion he had hoped for. Before he hit the water, the Lokhali on the bank had found their voices. By the time he had surfaced, they were being reinforced by other warriors from the village.

Another spear plunged into the river quite near

to him, and then another. A few powerful strokes brought him to the woman. There was no time to try to discover who she was.

"Turn on your back!" he yelled. "I'll tow you!"

Obediently, she turned over. He grasped her under the armpits and with rapid, nervous kicks propelled them both back to the barge. Suddenly, he felt a blow, and the woman shuddered, letting out a great sigh. He paid no attention to it, being intent only on getting them both to the comparative safety of the barge.

Somehow, he got her there.

As Shon Hu hauled her aboard, he saw the short spear that was sticking in her stomach and the dark rivulet of blood that pulsed over her brown flesh.

Then he hauled himself aboard and knelt there, panting with exertion, gazing at the contorted but still recognizable features of Ann.

"Get it out!" she hissed. "For God's sake get it out!"

Then she fainted.

# THIRTY-FIVE

IT WAS SHON HU WHO took the spear out. Paul was trembling and crying and useless. And it was Zu Shan and Nemo who, between them, somehow managed to keep the barge on a steady course and pole it safely out of range of the Lokhali spears and away from the village.

Paul managed to pull himself together before she opened her eyes.

"You were right, after all," she murmured. "It was an appointment in Samara, wasn't it?"

For a moment, he didn't know what she meant. Then it all came back to him. The *Gloria Mundi*. Champagne on the navigation deck after they had plugged the meteor holes. Philosophizing and speculating about Altair. Then Ann had told him about Finagle's Second Law. And he had told her the legend of an appointment in Samara.

"Ann, my dear . . . My dear." He looked at her helplessly. "You're going to be all right."

With an effort, she raised herself up from the little pillow of skins that Shon Hu had managed to slip under her head. Paul supported her while she studied the wound in her stomach with professional interest.

"It doesn't hurt much, now," she said calmly. "That's not a good sign. Some veinous blood, but no arterial blood . . . That's a bit of help . . . But I'm afraid I'm going to die . . . It may take time . . . You'll have to help me, Paul. I may get terribly thirsty . . . Normally, I wouldn't prescribe much liquid, but in this case it doesn't matter . . . Of course, if you can plug it without hurting me too much, you'll slow down the loss of blood."

She leaned against him, exhausted. Gently, he lowered her to the pillow.

"Any old plug will do," gasped Ann. "A piece of cloth, a piece of leather—anything."

He tore a strip of musa loul, made it into a wad and tried to press it into the gaping wound.

Ann screamed.

Shon Hu made a sign to Zu Shan and drew his pole back into the barge.

He came and squatted by Ann, regarding her objectively. Then he turned to Paul. "Lord, what does the woman need?"

"I have to press this into her wound," explained Paul. "But—but it hurts too much."

"Lord, this can be accomplished. Do what must

be done when I give the sign."

Expertly, Shon Hu placed his hands on each of Ann's temples and pressed gently but firmly. For a moment or two, she struggled pitifully, not knowing what was happening. Then suddenly her eyes closed and her body became slack.

Shon Hu nodded and took his hands away. Paul pressed the wad firmly into the wound. Presently Ann opened her eyes.

"I thought you must have gone back home, back to Earth," she murmured faintly. "It was the one satisfaction I had . . . Every night, I'd say to myself: Well, at least Paul hasn't come unstuck. He's on his way back home . . . What happened to the *Gloria Mundi*?"

"It blew itself up, according to the destruction programme, after the three of us left it to go and look for you and the others."

Ann coughed painfully and held Paul's hand tightly, pressing it to her breast. When the spasm was over, she said: "So the voyage has ended in complete disaster . . . What a waste it's all been—what a terrible waste."

"No, it hasn't," said Paul, then he looked down at her pain-twisted face and realized the stupidity of his remark. He began to stroke her white hair tenderly. "Forgive me. I'm a fool. But, Ann, I've discovered something so incredibly wonderful that—that it would seem to make any tragedy worthwhile . . . That's a damnfool thing to say—but it's true."

She tried to smile. "You must tell me about your wonderful discovery . . . I would like very much to think that it's all been worthwhile."

"You should rest. Try to sleep . . . You mustn't talk."

"I'll be able to sleep quite soon enough," she said grimly. "And you can do most of the talking . . . Now tell me about it."

As briefly as he could, he told her about his capture by the Bayani and of the friendship that had developed between himself and Enka Ne, otherwise Shah Shan. He told her about Oruri, the ultimate god of the Bayani. Then, passing quickly over much that had happened since the death of Shah Shan, he told her of Nemo's dreams, the legend of the coming, and how he finally made the journey to the Temple of the White Darkness. And, finally, he told her of his discovery of and encounter with the *Aru Re*.

Sometimes, while he was talking, Ann closed her eyes and seemed to drift off into unconsciousness. He was not quite sure how much she heard of his story—or, indeed, whether she could make much sense of it. But he went on talking desperately, because if she were not unconscious but only dozing, she might miss the sound of his voice.

As he talked, everything began to seem utterly unreal to him. He had never found the *Aru Re*. He was not even here on a barge, drifting on a dark river through a primeval forest, talking to a dying woman. He was dreaming. Probably, he was still in suspended animation aboard the *Gloria Mundi*—and his spirit was rebelling, by creating its own world of fantasy, against that unnatural state that had nothing to do with either living or dying. And presently, he would be defrozen. And then he would become fully alive.

Suddenly, he realized that he had stopped talking and that Ann had opened her eyes and was looking at him.

"Yes, I think you're right," she said faintly, "It's been worthwhile . . . I—I'm not sure I've got it all clearly in my head—my mind isn't working too well. But if the part about the *Aru Re* means what I think, you've made the most wonderful discovery in all the ages . . . Oh, Paul . . . I'm so—so . . . " her voice trailed away.

There were tears running down his face. "But I've got no one to tell it to," he burst out desperately, "no one, but—" he stopped.

"But a dying woman?" Ann smiled. "Stay alive, Paul. Just stay alive . . . I'm afraid you've got the harder job."

He bent and kissed her forehead. Great beads of sweat were forming on it. But the flesh was sadly cold.

"I wish—oh, God, I wish I knew what happened to the others!"

If Ann had survived—at least until his stupid Galahad act—why could not some of the others have survived? If he could find them, no matter what happened afterwards, at least he would have human company. No! That was a bloody silly thing to think. He already had Zu Shan, Nemo, Shon Hu. All good, very good, human company. But still alien. Human but alien. Strangers on the farther shore . . .

"You have accounted for three," said Ann in a weak voice. I'm . . . so—so sorry, Paul. But I can account for the rest . . . It was on that very first night after we left the *Gloria Mundi*." She laughed faintly, but the laughter degenerated into a fit of coughing that hurt her badly; and it was some time before she could continue. "You remember we went to look for the Swedish, French and Dutch pairs . . . It was a long time before I found what happened to them, but I'll tell you about that in a minute . . . Oh, God, Paul! We were so sure of ourselves—so clever! We were scientists. We had weapons. We had intelligence. The only thing we didn't have was the thing we really needed—forest lore . . . We were so confident—such easy game . . . The three of us walked straight into a hunting party of these forest people—they call themselves the Lokh. We didn't even fire a shot. They had us stripped of everything—all lovely equipment just tossed away by savages—and trussed like turkeys in a matter of seconds . . . The Italian girl wouldn't stop screaming, so they killed her . . . They weren't being brutal. It was just their idea of self-preservation. They didn't want to attract our friends, if any, or dangerous animals . . . Lisa—you remember Lisa?—she was very calm. But for her, I'd probably gone the same way as Franca. But she made me keep still and quiet—no matter what they did to us . . . They weren't cruel, just inquisitive . . . We must have really baffled them . . . Anyway, they took us back to the village. They kept us prisoners for a while. Then we began to pick up some of the language. We tried to explain to them how we had come to Altair Five. But it was no use. They just refused to believe it . . . After a time, they let us have our freedom—more or less. After all, there was nowhere to go. We just didn't

have enough strength or knowledge . . . Poor Lisa.
She poisoned herself . . . She just went round
eating every damn fruit, flower or root she could
find until she got something that did the trick. The
Lokh didn't know what she was up to. They
thought it was very funny. She was the joke of the
village . . . As for me, it seems ridiculous now, but I
still found life very dear. So I just tried to make
myself useful about the place . . . I began playing
doctor—treating wounds, setting bones, that sort
of thing . . . I think they got to like me . . . And that's
how it was until you came. The days just ran into
one another. And there wasn't any past, and there
wasn't any future. At one time, I thought I was
going mad . . . But I wasn't . . . And that's all . . .
And now it's ending like this.'' She smiled.
''Finagle's Second Law—remember?''

Paul lifted her hand and kissed it. ''Oh, my love.
My poor love.''

''Oh, yes, I was going to tell you about the
others,'' she said. ''The Stone Age got them. Isn't
that a joke? They had enough fire power to destroy
an army, and the Stone Age got them.''

He looked at her, puzzled.

''I'm sorry,'' murmured Ann. ''I'm not being
very coherent . . . There are some pretty dreadful
beasts in the forest, and the Lokh protect their
village by digging a ring of camouflaged pits
around it. The camouflage is very good. I've
nearly fallen into the damn things, myself . . . They
have these pits, with sharpened stakes sticking up
in them, in various parts of the forest. Every now
and then they go out to inspect them and see what
they have caught . . . They took me out to one of

the pits one day. There was some plastic armour, sweeper rifles, transceivers and—and six skeletons at the bottom . . . The twenty-first century defeated by the Stone Age . . . The Lokh thought they were being kind showing me what had happened to my companions . . . That was when I thought I might go mad.''

''Ann,'' he said, gently wiping the sweat from her forehead and feeling the terrible coldness again, ''I'm a fool—an absolute fool. I shouldn't have let you talk, Please, *please* rest now.''

''Sooner than you think,'' she murmured. ''Much . . . sooner than you think . . . Don't reproach yourself, my dear.'' Her eyes were half-closed, and there was a faint smile on her lips. ''It was worth it to see . . . my husband . . . again . . . Caxton Hall, ten-thirty . . . A red rose . . . You looked rather sweet—and a bit frightened.''

She began to cough, and this time there was some blood. The paroxysm exhausted her, but there didn't seem to be pain any more.

''Not long now,'' she said thickly. ''I didn't expect to see it up top so soon . . . The blood . . . Hold me, Paul. Hold me . . . It's such a lonely business . . . Afterwards, the river . . . It's so lovely to think of everything being washed away . . . Washed clean.''

He lifted her body and held it close against him, stroking her hair—the soft white hair—mechanically, while the tears trickled down his face and mingled with the cold sweat on hers.

''My dear, my love,'' he sobbed desperately. ''You're not going to die, I'm not going to let you go . . . I'm not going to let you . . . I must think.

God, I must think . . . A dressing—that's it. A decent dressing. Then when we get to Baya Nor I'll—" he stopped.

There had been no sound, no sigh. No anything. She just hung slackly in his arms. He was talking to a dead woman.

For some time, he sat there motionless, holding her. Not thinking. Not seeing.

Presently, he was aware of Shon Hu's arm on his shoulder.

"Lord," said the Bayani gently, "she travels to the bosom of Oruri. Let her go in peace."

Presently, they made a shroud of skins for her, and weighted it with stones.

Presently, as she had wished, Ann Victoria Marlow, *née* Watkins, native of Earth, slipped back into a dark and cleansing river on the far side of the sky.

# THIRTY-SIX

PAUL MARLOWE STARED down at the sodden
ashes of what had once been his home, and felt
nothing but a great emptiness inside him. It was
like a cold black void that mysteriously seemed to
swell without exerting either pressure or pain. Too
much had happened in the last few days, he supposed, for him to feel anything now. Later, no
doubt, the numbness would go away and he would
be able to assimilate this final tragedy. He wondered, curiously and clinically, if the feeling would
be deep enough to move him to tears.

The journey back along the Watering of Oruri
and then the Canal of Life had been accomplished
safely without any further interference from man
or beast—at least, he supposed it had. For after

Ann's death, he had been too traumatized to pay much attention to what was going on. He had sat calmly on the barge, staring at and through the impenetrable green walls of the forest, while day merged into night and night merged into day once more. Shon Hu had taken command of the party, deciding when to rest and where to make camp. and Paul had been as obedient and docile as a child.

But as the barge came nearer to Baya Nor the shock began to recede. Slowly he emerged from the deadly lethargy that had gripped him. He began to think once again, realizing that despite privation and tragedy, the journey had been successful, that he had made the most important discovery in the history of mankind, and that he was on his way home. It was the realization of being on his way home that unnerved him a little. Home, originally, had been somewhere on Earth—and he couldn't clearly remember where. It was now on Altair Five—and he could visualize very clearly exactly where it was and what it was.

It was a thatched house, standing on short stilts. It was a small dark woman who was immensely proud of the growing bundle of life in her belly . . . It was a bowl of cooled kappa spirit on the verandah steps in the evening . . . It was the sound of bare feet against wood, the smell of cooking, the tranquil movements of a small alien body . . .

The barge was only a few hours' poling from Baya Nor before Paul had pulled himself together sufficiently to think about Enka Ne. In making his journey to the Temple of the White Darkness, he had not only challenged the authority of the god-king, he had humiliated him. He had humiliated Enka Ne by destroying the pursuing barge and by tipping the god-king's warriors into the Canal of Life.

Possibly, for the sake of his prestige, Enka Ne would choose to treat the incident as if it had never happened. But that, thought Paul, was unlikely. It was far more likely that, as soon as he was able, Enka Ne would inflict some punishment or humiliation in return.

That was why Paul had not allowed Shon Hu and Zu Shan to bring the barge back to the city. He had made them stay with it on the Canal of Life, about an hour's walking distance away, while he came on ahead to learn—if he could—something of the situation. If he did not return that day, he had left them with orders to go back into the forest for a while, in the hope that time would diminish the god-king's displeasure and that he, Paul, would be able to establish sole responsibility for his transgression.

It had been raining during the night, but the day was becoming very warm, and the earth was steaming. And now, here he was, staring at an untidy scattering of damp ashes, patiently watched by the child, Tsong Tsong, whom Paul had left as company for Mylai Tui.

Tsong Tsong was as wet and miserable as the ashes. He had never been particularly bright or coherent, and he was now an even more pathetic figure, being half-starved. It had been the desire of his master, Poul Mer Lo, that Tsong Tsong should stay at the house. The child had interpreted the command literally and, even after the house had been burned down and Mylai Tui was dead, Tsong Tsong had kept vigil—patiently waiting for the return of Poul Mer Lo.

If Paul had never come back, he reflected, no doubt Tsong Tsong would have stayed there until he died of starvation..

He patted the small boy's head, looked down with pity at the blank face, the dark uncomprehending eyes, and patiently elicited the story.

"Lord," said Tsong Tsong in atrociously low Bayani, "it was perhaps the morning of the day after you went on the great journey . . . Or the morning of the day after that day . . . I have been hungry, lord, and I do not greatly remember these things . . . There were many warriors. They came from the god-king . . . It was a good morning because I had eaten much meat that the woman, Mylai Tui, could not eat . . . She was a good cook, lord, though cooking seemed to make her weep. Perhaps the vapours of the food were not good to her eyes . . . But the meat was excellent."

"Tsong Tsong," said Paul gently, "you were telling me about the warriors."

"Yes, lord . . . The warriors came . . . They made the woman leave the houe. She was angry and there were many loud words . . . I—I stood back, lord, because it is known that the warriors of Enka Ne are impatient men. So, being unworthy of their consideration, and also much afraid, I drew back . . . My lord understands that it would perhaps not have been good for me to remain?"

"Yes, I understand. Tell me what happened."

"The warriors said they must burn the house, and this I could not understand, because it is known that Poul Mer Lo is of some importance . . . It was very strange, lord. When the woman, Mylai Tui, saw them make fire she became as one touched by Oruri. She shook and spoke in a loud voice and wept . . . She tried to run into the burning house, shouting words that I could not understand. But a warrior held her. It was very frightening, lord . . . And the house made great noisy flames. And then she seized a trident and wounded the man who held her . . . And then—and then she died.''

Paul was amazed that he could still find no tears, no pain.

He knelt down and rested his hand on the small boy's shoulder. "How did she die, Tsong Tsong?" he asked calmly.

The boy seemed surprised at the question. "A warrior struck her."

"It was—it was quick?"

"Lord, the warriors of Enka Ne do not need to strike twice . . . I have been very hungry since then. There was some kappa, but it was black and had the taste of fire about it. My stomach was unhappy . . . Forgive me, lord, but do you have any food?"

Paul thought for a moment or two. Then he said: "Listen carefully, Tsong Tsong. There is something that you must do, then you shall have much food . . . Do you think you can walk?"

"Yes, lord, but it not a thing I greatly desire to do."

"I am sorry, Tsong Tsong. It is necessary to walk to get to the food. I have left Shon Hu, the hunter, and your comrades Zu Shan and Nemo in the barge some distance from here along the Canal of Life. You must go to them. Tell them what you have told me. Also tell them that Poul Mer Lo desires that they and you shall remain in the forest for as many days as there are fingers on both hands. Can you remember that?"

"Yes, lord . . . Do they have much food?"

"Enough to fill you up, little one. Shon Hu is a good hunter. You will not starve. Now go—and say to them also that when they leave the forest they must be careful how they come to Baya Nor, and careful how they enquire after me."

The child stretched his limbs and gave a deep sigh. "I will remember, lord . . . You are not angry with me?"

"No, Tsong Tsong, I am not angry. Go, now, and soon you will eat."

He watched the small boy trot unsteadily down to the Canal of Life and along its bank. Then he turned to look at the steaming ashes once more.

He thought of Mylai Tui, so proud of the son she would never bear, and of Ann, enduring patiently in the heart of the forest until she could keep an appointment in Samara, and of the *Aru Re*, Bird of Mars, standing in its icy fastness through the passing millennia—a lofty, enigmatic sentinel waiting for the maturation of the seed.

So much had happened that he was drunk with privation and with grief and with wonder. The sun had not yet reached its zenith, but he was desperately tired.

He sat down on the small and relatively dry patch of earth that Tsong Tsong had vacated. For a while, he stared blankly at the ashes as if he expected Mylai Tui, phoenix wise, to rise from them. But there was nothing but silence and stillness.

After a time, he closed his aching eyes and immediately fell asleep—sitting up. Presently he toppled over, but he did not wake.

He did not wake until shortly before sunset. He was stiff and lonely and still filled with a great emptiness.

He looked around him and blinked. Then he sat up suddenly, oblivious of the throbbing in his head.

He was surrounded by a ring of tridents, and a ring of blank black faces of the warriors of the royal guard.

For a moment or two, unmoving, he tried to collect his thoughts. Obviously the warriors did not mean to kill him, for they could have accomplished that task quite easily while he was still sleeping. They looked, oddly, as if they were waiting for something.

He was debating in his mind what to say to them when he saw, through the descending twilight, a vehicle coming jerkily along the Road of Travail. At first he thought it was a cart. But then he saw that it was a palanquin, carried by eight muscular young girls. The equipage left the Road of Travail and came directly towards the ring of warriors.

Paul stood up, gazing at it in perplexity. He remembered the first time he had seen the shrouded palanquin that contained the oracle of Baya Nor. It had been on a barge on the Canal of Life, when Enka Ne, otherwise Shah Shan, was taking him to the temple of Baya Sur to witness the first of three sacrifices of girl children.

As if at a signal, the girls carrying the palanquin stopped and set it gently down. The curtains shrouding it did not move. But from inside there came a wild bird cry.

Then a thin and withered arm poked out from between the curtains, pointing unwaveringly at Paul. And an incredibly old yet firm voice said clearly: "He is the one!"

Dazed and exhausted still, Paul was aware of a great roaring in his ears. He felt the hands of the Bayani warriors catch him as he fell.

## THIRTY-SEVEN

HE WAS IN a darkened room, lit only by a few flickering oil lamps. A man with a white hood over his face peered at him through narrow eye-slits.

"Who are you?" The words came like gun-shot.

"I am Poul Mer Lo," Paul managed to say, "a stranger, now and always."

The man in the white hood stared at him intently. "Drink this." He held out a small calabash.

Obediently, Paul took the calabash and raised it to his lips. The liquid was like fire—fire that consumed rather than burned.

Something exploded in his head, and then he felt as if he were being dragged down into a maelstrom. And then he felt as if he were floating freely in space.

When he became conscious again, he realized vaguely that he was being supported by two guards.

"Who are you?" shouted the man in the white hood.

Paul felt an almost Olympian detachment. The situation was curious, but amusing. For all his aggressiveness, the man in the white hood was definitely dull-witted.

"I am Poul Mer Lo," repeated Paul carefully and with a little difficulty, "a stranger, now and always."

"Drink this," commanded the inquisitor. He held out the calabash.

Once more Paul took it and raised it to his lips. The fire flowed through his body, roaring and all-consuming. His thoughts became tongues of flame. A curtain of flame danced and drifted before his eyes, slowly burning itself away to reveal a great bird, covered in brilliant plumage, with iridescent feathers of blue and red and green and gold.

But the bird did not move. It had no head.

Once more the maelstrom dragged him down. Once more he felt as if he were floating freely in space. This time there were stars. They whirled about him as if he were the still pivot of a turning universe. The stars were whispering, and their message was important, but he could not hear the words. All he could do was to watch the speeding gyrations, the beautiful cosmic merry-go-round, until time itself drowned in the broad black ocean of eternity . . .

Until he was suddenly aware once more of a darkened room and a few flickering lamps. And a man with a white hood over his face.

The headless bird had disappeared. And yet . . . and yet he was still aware of its presence.

*"Who are you?"* The words rolled like waves, like thunder.

He did not know what to say, what to do, what to think, what to feel. He did not know what to believe; for identity had been lost and he seemed now to be nothing more than the vaguest thought of a thought.

*"Who are you?"* The waves crashed on the farther shore. The thunder rolled over a distant land.

And then came answering thunder.

And a voice from far, far away said: "There shall come a man among you, who yet has no power and whose power will be absolute. And because no man may wield such power, the man shall be as a king. And because none may live for ever, the king shall be as a god. Each year the king must die that the god may be reborn . . . Hear, now, the cry of a bird that has never flown . . . Behold the living god—whose name is Enka Ne!"

He listened to the voice in wonder, feeling the words beat upon him like hammer blows. He listened to the words and submitted to the voice—knowing at last that it was his. He moved, and there was a strange rustling. He looked down at the blue and gold feathers covering his arms.

From somewhere another voice, old and high and thin, uttered a wild bird cry. "He is the one!"

Then the man in the white hood cried: "Behold the living god!" And sank down to prostrate himself at the feet of one who had once been known by the name of Poul Mer Lo.

# THIRTY-EIGHT

AFTERWARDS HE HAD rested for a while in an apartment in the Temple of the Weeping Sun, guarded only by a single warrior. The ceremonial plumage had been removed, and the god-king now wore a simple samu, indistinguishable from those worn by thousands of his subjects.

The apartment—whose walls and floor and roof were of highly polished stone, veined, like a rich marble, with streaks of blue and red and green and gold—was not luxuriously furnished. But, compared to the simple furnishings of a thatched house that had stood once near to the Canal of Life, these furnishings were indeed those of a palace.

The foot and head of the couch on which he had rested were of black wood inlaid with copper. The

227

mattress consisted of multi-coloured Milanyl feathers held in a fine net of hair. Large translucent crystals hung from the ceiling, rotating slowly in the slight currents of air, transforming the lamplight emanating from several niches into a soft and mobile pattern.

The god-king yawned and stretched, looking about him for a moment or two. He was hungry. But there were more important matters than food.

He sent for Yurui Sa, general of the Order of the Blind Ones. The man in the white hood.

The warrior on guard heard the instructions of the god-king without either looking at him or making any verbal acknowledgement.

Presently, Yurui Sa entered the room. He stood stiffly, waiting. His gaze, like that of the warrior, remained fixed upon the ceiling.

"Oruri greets you, Yurui Sa."

"Lord, the greeting is a blessing."

"Sit down and be with me as with a friend, for there is much that I have to say to you."

"Lord," said the man pleadingly, "be merciful . . . I—I may not see you!"

"This, surely, needs explanation."

"So it has always been," went on Yurui Sa, "so it must always be. When the plumage has been put aside, the god-king may not be seen by men."

"So, perhaps, it has always been. But nothing endures for ever. When the plumage has been put aside, the god sleeps but the king still wakes. You may look upon the king, Yurui Sa. I have spoken."

"Lord, I am not worthy."

"Nevertheless—" and the voice was regal, the voice of Enka Ne "—nevertheless, it is my wish."

Slowly, Yurui Sa brought his gaze down from the ceiling. Enka Ne smiled at him, but there was fear on the face of the general of the Order of the Blind Ones.

"There will be some changes," said Enka Ne.

Yurui Sa let out a great sigh. "Yes, lord, there will be some changes."

"Now sit with me and tell me how it came to pass that one who was once Poul Mer Lo is now the god-king of the Bayani, though the time is not yet ripe for rebirth."

Yurui Sa swallowed uneasily. Then he sat down on the edge of the couch as if he expected the action to bring some terrible disaster.

Apparently, it did not. Thus heartened, he began to explain to Paul Marlowe, native of Earth, how it came about that he was destined to achieve god-head on Altair Five.

"Lord," said Yurui Sa, "much that is wonderful has happened, making the will of Oruri clear beyond question . . . Many days ago, it became known to one who now has no name that the stranger, Poul Mer Lo, intended to make a great journey. The knowledge was not received favourably. Therefore many warriors were despatched to end the journey before it had begun." Yurui Sa permitted himself a faint smile. "My lord may himself have some awareness of what happened on that occasion. The warriors failed to fulfil their task—and such warriors do not often fail in their duty. Their captain returned and, before dispatching himself to the bosom of Oruri, repeated the message given to him by Poul Mer Lo. That same day, one who now has no name suffered much pain in his chest, coughing greatly, and for a time being unable to speak. Thus was seen the first judgement of Oruri on one who perhaps had misinterpreted his will."

"You say he coughed greatly?"

"Yes, lord. There were many tears."

Paul's mind went back to the occasion of his only audience with Enka Ne the 610th. He remembered an old man—an old man weighed down with care and responsibility. An old man who coughed . . .

"Proceed with your story."

"Lord, even then there were those in the sacred city who were afflicted by strange thoughts. Some there were—myself among them—who meditated at length upon what had passed. Later, when warriors were sent to destroy the house of Poul Mer Lo, our meditations yielded enlightenment. Also, there was an unmistakable sign of the will of Oruri."

"What was this sign?"

"Lord, as the house burned, he who has no name was seized by much coughing. As the flames died, so died he who has no name. Thus was seen the second judgement of Oruri . . . Then the oracle spoke, saying that fire would awaken from the ashes . . . And so, lord, were you revealed to your people."

Paul Marlowe, formerly known as Poul Mer Lo, now Enka Ne the 611th, was silent for a few moments. He felt weary still—unutterably weary. So much had happened that he could not hope to assimilate—at least, not yet. He smiled grimly to himself. But there would be time. Indeed, there would be time . . .

And then, suddenly, he remembered about Shon Hu and the barge.

"When Poul Mer Lo came from the forest, he left certain companions waiting in a barge on the Canal of Life. I desire that these people—and a child who has by now reached them—be brought to Baya Nor unharmed."

"Lord, forgive me. This thing is already done. Warriors were instructed to watch for the coming of Poul Mer Lo. They have found the barge, its occupants and the boy who was despatched to meet them."

"None have been harmed?"

"Lord, they have been questioned, but none was harmed."

"It is well, Yurui Sa, for these are humble people, yet they have a friend who is highly placed."

The general of the Order of the Blind Ones fidgeted uncomfortably. "Lord, the hunter, Shon Hu, has said that Poul Mer Lo has held converse with Oruri, also that he has looked upon the form . . . Forgive me, lord, but can this be so?"

"It is no more than the truth."

"Then is my heart filled with much glory, for I have spoken with a great one who has himself spoken with one yet greater . . . Permit me to withdraw, lord, that I may dwell upon these wonders."

"Yurui Sa, the wish is granted. Now send to me these people who journeyed with Poul Mer Lo. Send also much food, for these, my guests, will be hungry . . . And remember. There will be some changes."

The general of the Order of the Blind Ones stood up. Again he sighed deeply. "These things shall be done. And, lord, I will remember that there will be some changes."

Enka Ne leaned back upon the couch.

The warrior guarding him continued to stare fixedly at the ceiling.

## THIRTY- NINE

IT WAS A WARM, CLEAR evening. Paul Marlowe, clad only in a worn samu, sat on the bank of the Canal of Life not far from the Road of Travail; and not far, also, from a patch of ground where ashes had been covered by a green resurgence of grass. Theoretically, he had thirty-seven days left to live.

It was not often these days that he could find time to put aside the *persona* of Enka Ne. There was so much to do, so much to plan. For, since greatness had been thrust upon him, he had become a one-man renaissance. He had seen it as his task to lift the Bayani out of their static, medieval society and to stimulate them into creative thought. Into attitudes that, if they were allowed to flourish, might one day sweep the people of Baya

Nor into a golden age where science and technology and tradition and art would be fused into a harmonious and evolving way of life.

The task was great—too great for one man who had absolute power only for a year. Yet, whatever came afterwards—or whoever came afterwards—a start had to be made. And Paul Marlowe's knowledge of human history was such that he could derive comfort from the fact that, once the transformation had begun, it would take some stopping.

And it had certainly begun. There was no doubt about that.

Schools had been established. First, he had had to teach the teachers; but the work was not as difficult as he had anticipated, because he had absolute authority and the unquestioning services of the most intelligent men he could find. They were willing to learn and to pass on what they had learned—not because of burning curiosity and a desire to expand their horizons but simply because it was the wish of Enka Ne. Perhaps the curiosity, the initiative and the enthusiasm would come later, thought Paul. But whether it did or not in this generation, the important fact remained: schools had been established. For the first time in their history, the children of the Bayani were learning to read and write.

Dissatisfied with the broad kappa leaves that he had previously used for paper, Paul had experimented with musa loul and animal parchment. Already he had set up a small 'factory' for the production of paper, various inks, brushes and quill pens. At the same time, he had commanded some of the priests who had become proficient in this strange new art of writing to set down all they could remember of the history of Baya Nor and its god-kings, of its customs, of its songs and legends and of its laws. Presently, there would be a small body of literature on which the children who were now learning to read could exercise their new talent.

In the realm of technology there had been tremendous advances already. The Bayani were were skilled craftsmen and once a new principle had been demonstrated to them, they grasped it quickly—and improved upon it. Paul showed them how to reduce friction by 'stream-lining' their blunt barges, so that the barges now cut their way through the water instead of pushing their way through it. Then he demonstrated how oars could be used more effectively than poles, and how a sail could be used to reduce the work of the oarsmen.

Now, many of the craft that travelled along the Bayani canals were rowing boats or sailing dinghies, moving at twice the speed with half the effort.

But perhaps his greatest triumph was the introduction of small windmills, harnessed to water-wheels, for the irrigation of the wide kappa fields. So much manpower—or womanpower—was saved by this innovation, that the Bayani were able to extend the area of the land they cultivated, grow richer crops and so raise the standard of living.

Perhaps the most curious effect of Paul's efforts was that he seemed to have created a national obsession—for kite-flying. It rapidly became the most popular sport in Baya Nor. It attracted all ages, including the very old and the very young.

Once they had grasped the principle, the Bayani developed a positive genius for making elaborate kites. They were far superior to anything that Paul himself could have built. Some of the kites were so large and so skilfully constructed that, given the right kind of wind conditions, they could lift a small Bayani clear of the ground. Indeed, one or two of the more devoted enthusiasts had already been lifted up or blown into the Mirror of Oruri for their pains.

The Bayani seemed to have a natural understanding of the force of the wind as they had of the force of flowing water. Already, a few of the more experimental and adventurous Bayani were building small gliders. It would be rather odd, thought Paul, but not entirely surprising if they developed successful heavier-than-air machines a century or two before they developed engines.

But there were other, more subtle changes that he had brought about and with which he was greatly pleased. Except as a punishment for murder and crimes of violence, he had abolished the death penalty. He had also completely abolished torture. For 'civil' cases and minor offences such as stealing, he had instituted trial by jury. Major offences were still tried by the god-king himself.

The one Bayani institution that he would have liked most to destroy he did not feel secure enough to destroy. It was human sacrifice—of which he himself would presently become a victim.

The Bayani had already seen many of their most ancient customs and traditions either modified or abolished. On the whole, they had reacted to change remarkably well—though Paul was acutely aware of the existence of a group of 'conservative' elements who bitterly resented change simply because things had always been done thus. At present the discontents were disorganized. They muttered among themselves, but still continued to adhere strictly to the principle of absolute loyalty to their absolute ruler.

If, however, they were pushed too far—as, for example, by the abolition of human sacrifice, a concept to them of fundamental religious importance—they could conceivably unite as a 'political' group. The one thing that Paul was determined to avoid was any danger of rebellion or civil war. It would have destroyed much of the progress that had been made so far. If successful, it might even have brought about a 'burning of the books' before books had had time to prove their intrinsic worth.

One thing was sure, because of the intrusion of a stranger who had risen to absolute power the civilization of Baya Nor could never again be static. It must go forward—or back.

So, in order to give his one-man renaissance the best possible chance of flourishing, Paul felt that he would have to leave human sacrifice alone. After all, it did not affect more than twenty people a year—most of them young girls—and the victims were not only willing to accept martyrdom, but competitively willing. It was a great distinction. For they after all, were the beloved of Oruri.

There was, of course, one potential victim who did not have such a comforting philosophy. And that was Paul himself. He wondered how he would feel about the situation in another thirty-seven days. He hoped—he hoped very much—that he would be able to accept his fate as tranquilly as Shah Shan had done. For, in the Bayani philosophy, it was necessary that one who knew how to live should also know how to die.

As he sat by the bank of the Canal of Life, reviewing the happenings of the last few months, Paul Marlowe was filled with a deep satisfaction. A start had been made. The Bayani were beginning their long and painful march from the twilight world of medieval orthodoxy towards an intellectual and an emotional sunrise. A man's life was not such a high price for the shaping of a new society . . .

Paul sat by the Canal of Life for a long time. It was on such an evening as this, when the nine small moons of Altair Five swarmed gaily across the sky, that he had been wont to sit upon the verandah steps drinking cooled kappa spirit and philosophizing in words that Mylai Tui could not understand.

He thought of her now with pleasurable sadness, remembering the baffling almost dog-like devotion of the tiny woman who had once been a temple prostitute, who had taught him the Bayani language and who had become to all intents and purposes his wife. He thought of her and wished that she could have lived to bear the child of whose conception she had been so proud. He wished that she could have known also that Poul Mer Lo, her lord, was destined to become the god-king. Poor Mylai Tui, she would have exploded with self-importance—and love . . .

Then he thought of Ann, who was already becoming shadowy again in his mind. Dear, remote, elusive Ann—who had once been a familiar stranger. Also, his wife . . . It was nearly a quarter of a century since they had left Earth together in the *Gloria Mundi* . . . He had, he supposed, aged physically not much more than about six years in all that time. But already he felt very old, very tired. Perhaps you could not cheat Nature after all, and there was some delayed after-effect to all the years of suspended animation. Or maybe there was a simpler explanation. Perhaps he had merely travelled too far, seen too much and been too much alone.

The night was suddenly crowded with ghosts. Ann . . . Mylai Tui . . . An unborn child . . . Shah Shan . . . And a woman with whom he had once danced the Emperor Waltz on the other side of the sky . . .

He looked up now at this alien sky whose constellations had become more familiar to him than those other constellations of long ago.

He looked up and watched the nine moons of Altair Five swinging purposefully against the dusty backcloth of stars.

And his heart began to beat in his chest like a mad thing.

He counted the moons carefully, while his heart pumped wildly and his arms trembled and his eyes smarted.

He took a deep breath and counted them again.

There were now ten tiny moons—not nine. Surely that could only mean one thing . . .

Dazed and shaking, he began to run back to the sacred city—back to the private room where he still kept his battered, and so far useless, transceiver.

# FORTY

HE STOOD ON THE small, high balcony of the Temple of the Weeping Sun. His eyes were fixed on the cluster of moons already approaching the horizon. There were still ten.

The transceiver was in his hand, its telescopic aerial extended.

He was still shaking, and sweat made his fingers slip on the tiny studs of the transceiver as he set it for transmission at five hundred metres on the medium wave band. If the tenth moon of Altair Five was indeed a star ship—and what an unlikely *if* that was!—orbiting the planet, surely an automatic continuous watch would be kept on all wave bands. But if it was a star ship, how the devil could it be a terrestrial vessel? It had arrived at

Altair Five less than three years after the *Gloria Mundi*. Yet, when the *Gloria Mundi* had left Earth, apart from the American and Russian vessels, no other star ships—so far as Paul knew—had even left the drawing board. On the other hand, if it wasn't a terrestrial vessel, what else could it be? A large meteor that had wandered in from deep space and found an orbital path? A star ship from another system altogether?

Paul's head was a turmoil of possibilities, impossibilities and plain crazy hopes.

"Please, God, let it be a ship from Earth," he prayed as he pressed the transmit stud on the transceiver. "Please, God, let it be a ship from Earth—and let this bloody box work!"

Then he said, in as calm a voice as he could manage: "Altair Five calling orbiting vessel. Altair Five calling orbiting vessel. Come in, please, on five hundred metres. Come in, please, on five hundred metres. Over . . . Over to you."

He switched to receive and waited, his eyes fixed hypnotically on the ten small moons. There was nothing—nothing but the sound of a light breeze that rippled the surface of the Mirror of Oruri. Nothing but the stupid, agitated beating of his heart.

He switched to transmit again. "Altair Five calling orbiting vessel. Altair Five calling vessel. Come in, please, on five hundred metres. Come in, please, on five hundred metres. Over to you."

Still nothing. Presently the moons would be over the horizon, and that would be that. Maybe they were already out of range of the small transceiver. Maybe the damn thing wasn't working, anyway. Maybe it was an extra-terrestrial ship and the occupants didn't bother to keep a radio watch because they were all little green men with built-in telepathic antennae. Maybe it was just a bloody great lump of rock—a cold, dead piece of space debris . . . Maybe . . . Maybe . . .

At least the receiving circuits were working. He could now hear the hiss and crackle of static—an inane message, announcing only the presence of an electrical storm somewhere in the atmosphere.

"Say something, you bastard," he raged. "Don't just hook yourself on to a flock of moons and go skipping gaily by . . . I'm alone, do you hear? Alone . . . Alone with a bloody great family of children, and no one to talk to . . . Say something, you stupid, tantalizing bastard!"

And then it came.

The miracle.

The voice of man reaching out to man across the black barrier of space.

"This is the *Cristobal Colon* calling Altair Five." The static was getting worse. But the words—the blessed, beautiful words—were unmistakable. "This is the *Cristobal Colon* calling Altair Five . . . Greetings from Earth . . . Identify yourself, please. Over."

For a dreadful moment or two he couldn't speak. There was a tightness in his chest, and his heart seemed ready to burst. He opened his mouth and at first there was only a harsh gurgling. Instantly—and curiously—he was ashamed. He clenched his fist until the nails dug into his palms, and then he forced out the words.

"I'm Paul Marlowe," he managed to say. "The only survivor—" his voice broke and he had to start again. "The only survivor of the *Gloria Mundi* . . . When—when did you leave Earth?"

There was no answer. With a curse, he realized that he had forgotten to switch to receive. He hit the button savagely, and came in on mid-sentence from a different voice.

"—name is Konrad Jurgens, commander of the *Cristobal Colon*," said the accented voice slowly in English. "We left Earth under faster than light drive in twenty twenty-nine, four subjective years ago . . . We are so glad to discover that you are still alive—one of the great pioneers of star flight. What has happened to the *Gloria Mundi* and your companions? We have seen the canals but have not yet made detailed studies. What are the creatures of this planet like? Are they hostile? How shall we find you?"

Paul's eyes were on the moons, now very low in the sky. Somehow, he managed to keep his head.

"Sorry, no time for much explanation," he answered hurriedly. "You will soon be passing over my horizon, and I think we'll lose contact. So I'll concentrate on vital information. If you take tele-photo detail surveys of the area round the canals, you will see where the *Gloria Mundi* touched down . . . We burned a swathe through the forest—about ten kilometres long. It's probably visible even to the naked eye from a low orbit . . . You'll see also the crater where the *Gloria Mundi* programmed its own destruction after being abandoned. Touch down as near to it as possible. I'll send people out to meet you—you'll recognize them. But don't—repeat don't—leave the star ship until they come. There are also people in these parts who are not too friendly . . . I'll get the reception committee to meet you about two days from now . . . They are small, dark and quite human." He laughed, thinking of what he had learned from the *Aru Re*. "In fact, I think you are going to be amazed at how very human they are. Over to you."

"Message received. We will follow your instructions. Are you in good health? Over."

Paul, drunk with excitement, laughed somewhat hysterically and said: "I've never felt better in my life."

There was a short silence. Then he heard: "*Cristobal Colon* to Paul Marlowe. We have received your message and will follow your instructions. Are you in good health? Over."

Paul saw the ten moons disappearing one by one over the horizon. He tried to reach the *Cristobal Colon* again, and failed. He switched back to receive.

"*Cristobal Colon* to Paul Marlowe. We will follow your instructions. We no longer hear you. We will follow your instructions. We no longer hear you . . . *Cristobal Colon* to Paul Marlowe. We will follow—"

He switched off the transceiver and gave a great sigh.

The impossible seemed oddly inevitable, somehow—after it had happened.

He stood on the balcony of the Temple of the Weeping Sun for a long time, gazing at the night sky, trying not to be swamped by the torrent of thoughts and emotions that stormed inside him.

Faster than light drive . . . That was what they had said . . . Faster than light drive . . . Four subjective years of star flight . . . The *Cristobal Colon* must have left Earth seventeen years after the *Gloria Mundi* . . . . . And now here it was, orbiting Altair Five less than three years after the *Gloria Mundi* had touched down . . . Probably half the crew of this new ship were still at school when he was spending years in suspended animation on the long leap between stars . . . No wonder they regarded him as one of the pioneers of star flight . . . *Cristobal Colon* — a good name for a ship that, like Columbus, had opened up a new route for the voyagings of man . . . Soon, soon he would be speaking to men who could remember clearly what spring was like in London, or Paris or Rome. Men who still savoured the taste of beer or lager, roast beef and Yorkshire pudding or Frutti del Mare. Men—and, perhaps women—whose very looks and way of speaking would bring back so much to him of all that he had left behind—all that he had missed—on the other side of the sky . . .

Suddenly, the tumult in his head spent itself. He was desperately tired, exhausted by hope and excitement. He wanted only to sleep.

# EPILOGUE

ENKA NE SAT pensively on his couch. The single
Bayani warrior on guard stared fixedly at the ceiling. The *Cristobal Colon* had touched down successfully and its occupants had been met by a
troop of the god-king's personal escort. Besides
their tridents they had carried banners bearing the
legend: *Bienvenu, Wilkommen, Benvenuto, Welcome.* The troop had been led by a hunter, a boy
and a crippled child. It must, thought the god-king,
have been quite a carnival . . . And now men from
Earth walked in Baya Nor . . .

Yurui Sa, general of the Order of the Blind Ones,
entered the room and gazed upon the presence,
although the god-king wore only his samu.

"Lord, it is as you have commanded. The strangers wait in the place of many fountains . . . They are tall and powerful, these men, taller even than—" Yurui Sa stopped.

"Taller even," said the god-king with a faint smile, "than one who waited in the place of many fountains a long, long time ago."

During the past months, Yurui Sa and the god-king had developed something approaching friendship—but only in private, and when the plumage had been set aside. They were men of two worlds who had grown to respect each other.

"Lord," went on Yurui Sa, "I have seen the silver bird. It is truly a thing of much wonder, and very beautiful."

"Yes," said the god-king, "I do not doubt that it is very beautiful."

There was a short silence. Yurui Sa allowed his gaze to drift through the archway to the small balcony and the open sky. Soon the light would die and it would be evening.

"I think," said Yurui Sa tentatively, "that it would be very wonderful to journey in the silver bird to a land beyond the sky . . . Especially if one has already known that land, and if the heart has known much pain."

"Yurui Sa," said the god-king, "it seems that you are asking me a question."

"Forgive me, lord," answered Yurui Sa humbly, "I am indeed asking you a question—although the god-king is beyond the judgement of men."

The god-king sighed. Yurui Sa was asking Enka Ne what, until now, Paul Marlowe had dared not ask himself.

He stood up and walked through the archway, out on to the little balcony. The sun was low and large and red in the sky. It did not look much different from the sun that rose and set on an English landscape sixteen light-years away . . . And yet . . . And yet . . . It was different. Still beautiful. But different.

He thought of many things. He thought of a blue sky and puffy white clouds and cornfields. He thought of a small farmhouse and voices that he could still hear and faces that he could no longer visualize. He thought of a birthday cake and a toy star ship that you could launch by cranking a little handle and pressing the Go button.

And then he thought of Ann Marlowe, dying on a small wooden barge. He thought of Mylai Tui, proud because she was swollen with child. He thought of Bai Lut, who made a kite and brought about his own death, the destruction of a school, and a journey that led to the ironically amazing discovery that all men were truly brothers. And he thought of Shah Shan, with the brightness in his eyes—tranquil in the knowledge that his life belonged to his people . . .

The sun began to sink over the horizon. He stayed on the balcony and watched it disappear. Then he came back into the small room.

The god-king looked at Yurui Sa and smiled. "Once," he said softly, "I knew a stranger, Poul Mer Lo, who had ridden on a silver bird. Doubtless, he would have desired greatly to return to his land far beyond the sky . . . But—but I no longer know this man, being too concerned with the affairs of my people."

"Lord," said Yurui Sa, and his eyes were oddly bright, "I already knew the answer."

"Go, now," said Enka Ne, "for I must presently greet my guests."

A slight breeze came into the room, whispering softly through the folds of a garment that hung loosely on a wooden frame. The iridescent feathers shivered for a moment or two, and then became still.

# FRITZ LEIBER

# PHILIP K. DICK

| | |
|---|---|
| 15670 | **Dr. Bloodmoney or How We Got Along After the Bomb** $1.50 |
| 22386 | **Eye In The Sky** $1.25 |
| 27310 | **Game Players of Titan** 75¢ |
| 51910 | **The Man Who Japed** 95¢ |
| 76701 | **The Simulacra** $1.50 |
| 86050 | **Variable Man** $1.50 |
| 90951 | **The World Jones Made** $1.25 |

*Available wherever paperbacks are sold or use this coupon.*